WELCOME TO THE DOOM GAMES—

—*where a roll of a wizard's dice can save a princess or leave her captive to the evil Norx . . .*

—*where an apprentice cobbler with a speech impediment and a club foot can battle a Dark Lord with a ballpoint pen . . .*

—*where a talking cat and a ghostly mouse can start the multiverse crumbling around them . . .*

—*and where you'll encounter evil beasties galore, master sorcerers, beautiful but far from helpless maidens, lecherous dragons, rune stones that fight over the future, and a cosmic gameplayer who knows that rules are made to be broken. . . .*

thc dcstiny dice

"A delightful series that's sure to be a success."
—Robert Adams
    author of the HORSECLANS series

"Take one part T. H. White's *The Once and Future King*, two parts William Goldman's *The Princess Bride*, add a smidgen of Tolkien and a hefty helping of originality—including David Bischoff's penchant for felonious puns—and what do you have? Two things: *The Destiny Dice* . . . and a lot of fun."
—Joel Rosenberg
    author of the GUARDIANS OF THE FLAME series

Great Science Fiction from SIGNET

THE DESTINY DICE

BOOK ONE

of

THE GAMING MAGI

DAVID BISCHOFF

A SIGNET BOOK

NEW AMERICAN LIBRARY

NAL BOOKS ARE AVAILABLE AT QUANTITY DISCOUNTS WHEN USED
TO PROMOTE PRODUCTS OR SERVICES. FOR INFORMATION PLEASE
WRITE TO PREMIUM MARKETING DIVISION, NEW AMERICAN LIBRARY,
1633 BROADWAY, NEW YORK, NEW YORK 10019.

Cover art by Kinuko Craft

SIGNET TRADEMARK REG. U.S. PAT. OFF. AND FOREIGN COUNTRIES
REGISTERED TRADEMARK—MARCA REGISTRADA
HECHO EN CHICAGO, U.S.A.

SIGNET, SIGNET CLASSIC, MENTOR, PLUME, MERIDIAN AND NAL BOOKS
are published by New American Library,
1633 Broadway, New York, New York 10019

First Printing, March, 1985

1 2 3 4 5 6 7 8 9

PRINTED IN THE UNITED STATES OF AMERICA

For Mark
and Kerry,
both Bischoffs,
both brothers

pReface

two suns.

For centuries, this burning binary stared through the crisscross, the multitude of universes, sightless.

However, specified Time had intersected with foretold Space, and these eyelike suns opened their lids.

And these arcane orbs gazed.

Pupil incandescent with hatred, with purpose, glared from the sclera of hydrogen fusion. Solar flares leaped from hellish corneas, energized thought grasping through the interplay of bright and dark.

Beyond mere light and time, these thoughts summoned the cells. An unholy constellation formed, connected not by imaginary lines but by pure Will.

Of star clusters were the feet of this celestial body, slippered in shimmer; of star flows like pearlstrings were its arms, long enough to touch opposite ends of a galaxy.

White dwarfs, red giants, and neutron stars

with their attendant planets, streaking comets, silver moons, and barren asteroids composed the torso. The very debris of the voice crackled with the being's magic, marching now as a bloodstream of energy.

All this was clothed in stardust like glimmering silk, robing the light and the dark into one form. A grouping of quasars outlined the darkling cloak, ruffling like night over a fearful land to encompass nebulae with promised gloom.

In the creature's center, a black hole served as its heart.

Now these fiery eyes peered down past the flimsy veils that lined the universes. Piercing, penetrating, they searched. . . .

Searched until a mansion swathed in ivy and age was discovered. Past masonry walls the eyes peered, until they found the cluttered room.

The Being considered the occupants of this room briefly.

The notion flickered in its mind:

A mouse. Yes. With a mouse it shall all begin.

And now, with this thought, if waves of sound could carry across the vast gulfs between the galaxies, the gossamer walls betwixt existence and nonexistence, the universes would have filled with a chuckle.

chapter one

to begin with, a partial catalogue of a certain cluttered hall of legerdemain: one teak table; one crystalline decanter; one platinum tray; one pewter cup, half full of schnapps; one middle-aged magus, sipping the liquor to assuage his considerable tension.

The events of this next half hour were of crushing importance, the magus knew.

The man of magic wore muttonchop whiskers, immaculately shaven. His nose was perfectly formed, centered by a dimpled cleft; his cheeks were almost as high as the jut of thoughtful brow resting on upswept eyebrows. Look at the eyes, though. Riveting! Deep-set, one was bon-bon brown, the other the blue of a hopelessly azure sky.

Between sips, this sharp-dressed necromancer smoked a strong French cigarette, blowing the smoke toward a chandelier dangling from a frescoed ceiling.

Enter, stage left, a flash of movement.

A cat, silver and gold, dashed over portmanteaus, skipped over divans. Under rococo chairs and baroque sofa arms, it pattered up clouds of dust. The motes glimmered about the room's candles.

The cat's ears pricked high. It poised atop a rubble of books, stalking unseen quarry amid the floor fog. Green-flecked eyes glaring into the shadows, the feline seemed to gleam with feral delight, seemed to glow with smugness.

"Alabaster!" the magus called, his curls sweeping across the shoulders of his tweed topcoat as he turned his head. "Wretched cat. Naughty familiar. Haven't you learned? The mice are only ghosts here! Come. I need your company!"

Whiskers twitched at the Master's words. Lithely it leaped to the misty rug, padding under the table. The magus crushed his cigarette in the jaws of an alligator ashtray and bent to pick up his cat. The alligator licked its lips.

"There," the magus crooned as he situated the pile of soft fur upon his thin lap. "Isn't this much better than chasing tiny bits of ectoplasm, Alabaster?" he said, petting the tom.

The cat purred, rhythmically pushing, gently clawing the magus's waistcoat. A silver watch chain sparkled, and Alabaster batted it with a paw.

"Yes, dear one. What time is it exactly? Thank you for reminding me. I have been lost in contemplation and concentration." He plucked the watch from his pocket like a golden pill from its bottle. "Hmm. Almost time. Almost time, Alabaster. You go chase some dreams now, eh? I have to roll the dice."

Joinville tie bowing at his stiff collar, the man set the cat back on the rug, then pushed himself to his feet. He picked his cup from its tray, striking the decanter inadvertently.

It rang like a crystal chime.

The magus carried his cup to the Gaming Table, setting it upon the polished wood beside the Destiny Board. He dragged an oak chair around for his seat, then repaired to his workbench to obtain the magical articles he would need.

Oddments of the man's profession lay strewn in some obscure nonlinear order upon the long bench. Racked on a smudged wall stretched rows of pencil-labeled phials containing all manner of solids and liquids and colloids, like vivisected rainbows. Spider dust, dog urine. Dried human blood and camel mucus. Eldritch tomes lay haphazardly scattered hither and thither, most winged open, baring hand-lettered, illuminated pages brittle with age to the further indignities of exposure.

In bell jars beside the peeling wall hung pickled homunculi—leprechauns, pixies, fairies—their blinded eyes staring down upon the mortars and pestles, the scales and weights, the blackened Bunsen burners and the stained lab beakers. A cornucopia of sorcerous paraphernalia was stuffed, squirmed, and squeezed into every corner, every crevice and crack. Wands, talismans, crosses, and ankhs. Swastikas, grimoires, charms, and horrific masks. The odor hanging about seemed a compost of musk's malodor and perfume's sweetness; the mingled scents of good, evil, and the multitude of mixtures that compose life.

The fingers of the magus nimble rattled through the confusion toward a file box of shellacked pine. Tugging open a drawer, he withdrew a dusky velvet pouch, pinched closed with drawstrings. A moment's further search brought up a bulky brass candelabra bearing three candles, their sides and tarnished bases thick with waxy ooze. These articles the burdened magus lugged to the gaming table, muttering spells under his breath.

After perching the candelabra near the table edge, he plucked a flint light shaped like a human skull. He snapped this aflame. A long gout of fire leaped from sparks. The wicks lit, glittering weirdly with sparkles and clotted dazzles.

The magus opened the strings of the pouch. Within, swaddled by fabric, snuggled a pair of dice: ivory cubes, white with indented ebony dots. These he cupped into his palms as he examined the Destiny Board to study the situation.

The board itself was a relief map pasted on a russet-stained, sandpapered square of plywood. In the center of this map lay a perfect circle painted a subdued red. This circle radiated outward to cover the majority of board space. The remainder of the map was gray. Otherwise it seemed a normal map, representing mountains, lakes, an ocean, rivers—all the geological aspects of what appeared to be part of a continent.

Lending depth and shadowing, playing pieces stood scattered hither and yon upon the board in some contorted pattern. These were detailed replicas of castles and towers, cannon and cavalry, humans and nonhumans in such a wealth of variety and number that merely half again their number would completely crowd the chart. Frantically multicolored and multitudinous material composed the models: onyx and marble and brightly polished gold, glowing milk quartz, cut ivory and carved redwood speckled with diamonds. Prisms stationed randomly cast spectrums of light upon the scene, further confusing the mottled soup of hue, tint, and coruscation.

The magus focused his attention upon one section of the playing area, just short of the rust-red circle—in the slaty outlying lands. Before him lay a length of graph paper. With T-square, compass, and slide rule he computed, filling one corner of the blue sheet with hieroglyphics. Tongue peeking through lips, he completed his figuring, checked it for accuracy, then returned his attention to the area of impending importance.

Just off the line of demarcation stood a ceramic miniature, finished in glaze. Diminutive in comparison with the others, this piece showed its subject clothed in a long coppery cap, a scarf of some lavender shade, and an ankle-length ruffled flow of white. Mere inches from her loomed three larger pieces: three horses, topped with three fearsome, nonhuman creatures clutching tin swords.

This could be the crucial turning point, thought the magus. He increased his concentration. For a time he stared unblinking at the replicas paralyzed in some frieze of frenzied pursuit. Then he again checked his watch.

The moment drew near.

Sighting carefully, lining up for the throw, he cupped the smooth dice in his hand, squeezed them to get their feel once more, then rattled them to determine the proper balance for the toss. Breathing slowly, easily—all must be calm, all must be at rest—he lowered his eyes to the dotted cubes and muttered the appropriate chants and invocations indicated by his prefiguring.

All was ready. Only the roll itself actually remained.

The magus drew back his hand, lightly limbering his wrist. Such perfect control he felt! Such confidence that this day's work, despite its tension, its arduous preparation, would come to successful ends. Sighing, licking moisture over his dry lips, he commenced the forward movement of his arm to cast the dice of fate.

At the table's far edge, unseen by the magus, a snowy collection of ears and snout popped up, peering with pink eyes. Soundlessly, the creature scrabbled to perch upon the table, whip tail draping away into shadow. It sniffed the air hesitantly, then crawled forward on silent paws. Translucent, it moved like poorly contained smoke.

With a screech of ecstatic triumph, Alabaster the cat leaped upon the table. Its motion blurry-fast, it swiped at the creature with a paw. The startled mouse scrambled down the table, skirting the board edge, attracting the magus's attention. The cat jumped after it, shrilling frustrated fury.

"What?" The magus looked from the dice in his open palm to this inopportune interruption. "Alabaster, don't. . . !"

The ectoplasmic mouse scurried around the green-tinged base of the brass candelabra and soared off the table, almost floating away toward the floor. Alabaster lunged after it, banging the candelabra stalk as it too hurled into the air, off the table. The candelabra wobbled. The flames above the wicks trembled and sputtered— then the top-heavy mass of brass and wax and sorcerous fire toppled toward the magus.

The flames jetted across the man's arm, lighting the cloth. In a bat's blink, the burning raced to the shoulder of the tweed topcoat and brushed threateningly at silken locks.

The magus, yelping, bashed insanely at the lighted arm, letting the forgotten dice tumble where they might. The hand alone was insufficient; losing control of reason and caution, the man fell upon the table, snuffing the flames . . . but also jarring the playing board and game pieces into chaos. The candelabra had fallen to the floor. The magus stomped the fallen flames with his soles before they could spread to the rug.

Gulping in air, gasping it out, holding his burned arm, the magus staggered to lean in shock upon the playing table. He brushed his mussed hair from his eyes and looked, horrified, at the shambles of the board, then sought out the fallen dice.

They lay just at the edge of the board in the blue-colored area: the sea.

They lay within an inch of each other. Both their white, upraised surfaces held in their middle a single night black dot.

Snake eyes.

The magus stared disbelievingly at the dice for a moment. The implications and impending consequences of the botched throw sank into his mind. He fell back into his chair and muttered a groan, low and long.

Merde, he thought. This game was going to be a pisser.

chapter two

Ian Farthing was an idiot.

Not perhaps the way Mullshire folk seemed to think, all of them clucking over his physical imperfections, his speech impediment, and his feckless airs; rather he was an idiot because he thought himself such.

"Idiot!" he cried to himself as the toe of his boot snagged in a larch root, pitching him over a cliff.

A fine bold sun hung among scuds of cirrus in a cobalt sky, making the day gorgeous. This day was a fête day, a rites-of-spring day, back home. Ian had chosen to opt out. He'd decided to trek to the Dark Circle boundary where some gloom, some black sky, could be counted on, to match his mood.

It certainly wasn't his day.

The Mullshire lads would get falling-down drunk and tended to take random kicks and swings at good ol' Dungface, dear Duncetongue, lovely Eggneck if he got underfoot. Who needed a bear to bait if the Fart was about? The Idiot

17

didn't claw back. Besides, he moaned such bizarre cries, spasming like a beheaded chicken when you booted him proper, that 'twas such grand sport! There existed talk that the Idiot's parents should lease him out for just such occasions. A farthing to clobber Farthing! Har har! Bloody fine notion, that!

So today, even before the revelry had actually gotten underway in earnest, Ian Farthing had furtively snuck from his home, not telling ancient Mum nor Da what was afoot or where he was afoot to on this fine spring morn. Turree, turla, hey nonny and let the village scum find him out here! Yessir, a brisk limp out where they wouldn't venture, a day without work, might just bear some reward rather than the usual humiliation. So off through waving wheat, through grass aswish with wind, through bonny wood and sweet-flowered dale he had trod, mumbling to himself and wishing ardently that the earth would crack in twain and Perdition would swallow Turdy Scrivener and Moss Baker (damn their fat guts) and all the other lads who laughed at him.

Despite his clubfoot, because of the boot that Da, a cobbler by trade, had made him, Ian Farthing walked almost as fast as any man. Three miles he traipsed in surprisingly short time through forest and over hill, not stopping to listen to robins chirp or watch squirrel dances. No, he beelined for a view of the Dark Circle, the Black Land, the Magic Hole. Perhaps he would even have the nerve to cross the border today, he reasoned. A blasted heath, a boggy moor, misty, mushy, and full of fetidness! Just the thing! A fitting cobbler's son's holiday!

Hurrah!

The old limestone cliff offered a perfect view of the Dark Circle's crags and wastes. Ian, wanting badly to inhale a mordant view, had run to reach the knoll. The black roots of the larch, exposed by erosion, lay on the verge of this cliff; Ian had stood by this tree numberless times, and always he had watched his step. Now, though, he had lost the rhythm of movement and his footing because of what he saw on a hill beyond the Black Circle boundary.

Horses! Riders!

The closest was a single mount, the rider a swirl of copper, a smear of brown against the gray hill. The others were a group, perhaps a hundred yards behind the first, three splotches of black.

Astonishing!

At that moment he tripped . . .

. . . and hurtled headlong in a mad windmill tumble over the edge. He struck the slope hard and rolled in a half-conscious stupor the rest of the way. Bitter dirt in mouth. The sky spinning overhead (oh stupid Lumpneck, look what you've done to yourself now!). The grimy scent of limestone dust, the wrenching pain of repeated impact. Rocks against back, stones gouging at arms and legs, rocks biting cruelly at abdomen, at sides; rocks, stones, rocks, rocks, rocks! Ian landed in a skidding sprawl, slowed by a pile of dirt sprouting poison ivy. Amid leaves and stalks he lay dazed, arms and legs all akimbo like a marionette newly shorn of its strings. Breathing heavily, he was aware of a dull pain all over. Nothing sharp, nothing serious. Just lie here a moment, he instructed himself. Recover.

Then, with a scuffling, a bark, a hairy creature leaped upon him.

A slathering tongue licked his face.

Smell of dog.

Dog?

"Night?"

His vision was suddenly full of pitchy fur, floppy ear, lolling tongue. Worried brown eyes inquired behind a whine. Night's eyes.

"Why i' devil's name have you come piddlin' after me, cur?"

The animal barked. It wagged a tail that could have doubled for a mop. It smelled of rancid meat and sweat.

"Bleedin' purgatory, I wanna be alone. Told you that, beastie. What? Worried? Now wha' in God's land you worried about, doggie?"

With a plaintive "ruff!" the dog lifted its front paws onto Ian's coarse peasant's tunic, dribbling saliva. Night cocked his head in a soulful manner, then settled his sleek neck onto Ian's disheveled capuchon, penitent, contrite, yet concerned. "Worried I might fall, you mangy wolf-son? God's wounds! Bit late, don't you think?"

There was kindness, affection in the words;

words garbled and rendered mangled grunts, barely decipherable coagulations of vowels and consonants, ruined by a congenital distortion of Ian's upper palate. But the dog understood. Most beasts understood Ian Farthing. There seemed a strange affinity between the creatures of land and air and Ian—something the lad did not comprehend entirely. There was comfort to be had in any sort of understanding. And creatures like Night seemed to understand him far better than his fellow humans.

Except maybe for Hillary.

Night was not his dog. Night belonged to the knacker up Thin Way, in Needle Mews. Ian would often stop by the foul yard, full of pots and caldrons, bones and carcasses, to sit and pet Markson and knacker's mongrel and commune quietly with it. Sometimes the two took walks in the countryside, yapping and mumbling through the heath and moors, chasing the sighing wind. Today, though, Ian wanted nothing to do with any living, animate thing, so he had instructed the mutt to stay put among its master's bubbling fat and fertilizer, the furs, the hides, and soap.

"So now they'll think I've nabbed you. Hit me bloody good and proper anyways. With a cow's thighbone, no doubt. What am I going to do with you, eh? Pissing tailing my heels like this?"

Then he recalled what he had seen, what had caused him to forget his caution. "Holy Jesus, Night! Did you see what I saw up there?

Out on the Barrens, come out of Satan's arse like turds wi' wings!" Alarmed, the dog jumped to its feet, head low, growling. "Yah, right, mutt, I'll keep my distance, but I will have my looker 'bout. Coming this way they were!" He pointed past a stand of cedars that obscured the view. "I suppose we can muck through there—peek out. You game, laddie?"

The black dog crouched down, yapping querulously. "Christ's nails, yer a bit of a companion, you are." Ian stiffly rose and brushed off the dirt and dead leaf scraps clinging to the plain chausses on his legs. "Ain't gonna stick me nose in no dung, Night. Just want to see what's about, 'sall." He rearranged the capuchon, hooding his head. "See? We'll just creepy-creepy through yon twigs and prickly bushes, quiet as rats in wool stockings. Poke about awhile, you know. Probably won't see naught but deer spoor. C'mon, bitch spawn."

Ian struck out for the wood. At age twenty-three, working six and a half days a week banging at tacks, leather, and cloth for a couple of coins a month, he found life precious devoid of adventure, vicarious or otherwise. This morning might well prove to be an eyeful, and he most certainly was not going to cheat himself out of it because of a dumb dog's begging. No sir!

He crunched through the forest, trying to figure the best path through shrubs and vines. Soon, with a gruff bark, Night padded beside him, fur and ears abounce as though he were the gayest canine in the world. Ian smudged off a spot of dirt on the downy blond straggles he called whiskers and his da called arse fuzz. "That's more like it, Night. Long as you're here, we'll walk. Feel a bit all right already, I do."

His shoulder-length hair hung in clumps, a greasy blond frame to a pocked visage. The broken nose was aquiline, the lips seemed the hasty work of a dagger. Black eyebrows low on a wide brow gave him a brooding look, contributing a churlish aspect. Only the eyes betrayed intelligence; hazel eyes that sometimes gleamed with irony. His shoulders were stooped and crooked, and, together with his head and thick neck, make him as though he had been pulled from the womb by hearth tongs. His backbone was sharply curved, causing his abdomen and buttocks to protude unnaturally over stumpy legs. As he scuffed along now, his fingers twitched—faint echoes of the spastic fits which wracked his body at times. At five feet three inches, he stood inches shorter than most, and he lamented every inch. If he were only bigger, stronger, maybe he could corner his tormentors one by one in shadowed alleys and pound their unreasoning hatred from them.

Alas, his was not a fighting nature. Whether he was born without it or it had been beaten away, he'd no idea. Quite simply he wished no harm to any being . . . particularly his own being.

The shadows and deep green of the forest canopy shut out the sun as the young man and the dog moved through the mottled darkness, through gorse up to Ian's waist, and the familiar rustlings and earthy smells eased tensions. The forests and fields were his solace and comfort; his true home. What had he to fear among the woods, the leaves?

Fear.

The concept reminded him that he would do well to find a stick for protection. He was not permitted to carry normal weapons. "Like a knife to our throats that'd be!" an arbiter had proclaimed. "Who knows when one of his fits might cause harm to someone, just like ten year ago!"

That memory stirred a chord of dull pain for Ian. One morning he'd lost his mind with fury and tried to drown nasty taunting Tom Mounthole in a horse trough—the one time he had ever become violently offensive. Baron Richard had declared him possessed of a demon and tossed him into the claws of the doctors. These quacks had hired a barber first to let some blood, then to drill a small hole in his skull to release the evil spirit. The blood they had let; somehow, though, Ian managed to escape to the woods, where he hid for a month, living on roots and berries. When he finally returned to the fiefdom, he'd gone straight to Baron Richard and convinced the man his senses had returned in full measure; the demon was gone. But Richard had wagged a finger and warned that any further acts against normal folk by "you twisted gnome" would result in a certain skull-drilling.

Fortunately, he had learned to control his fits sufficiently that he attacked no one, no matter how provoked.

The thought of his fate if he did spurred a hand to his head, rubbing away a flicker of ache. The hand slipped down the neck, feeling the bumps that he hid with his hair. There were two of them, the exact same size, protruding like giant smooth pimples. They caused no discomfort, but were yet another ugliness to add to the overall tally, and Ian Farthing hated them. He was afraid to cut them off for fear of bleeding to death. As he touched them now, they seemed . . . warm. Abnormally warm. Ian shrugged and cast about for a stick.

Directly in his path, he found a quarterstaff-sized branch sprouting from a fallen tree, unrotted. A jump broke it off. Ian then stripped it of twigs. "There now," he said. "That'll be a lovely bone-cracker, Night. Don't you think?"

Night capered about, barking, then sniffed the new weapon suspiciously. Ian fell on the dog, hugging him. "Ah, Night! You're full of grand dreams, you are!" Playfully, Ian nuzzled Night's cold wet nose with his own, chuckled, and let the dog go. He continued his journey through the underbrush, batting offending branches away with his staff.

Ho ho! Through the deciduous timber, scruffing through smells and tastes. Fungus! Moss! Honeysuckle and wild cherry! Berries bloomed red, blue. Yes, much more like home than his parents' thatched roof and mud walls! One with the woods, he advanced.

The leafy ceiling broke up, allowing glimpses of the eternally bleak and stormy skies above the Dark Land. Ian Farthing whispered for Night to stay close.

At the edge of the forest, behind a yew, he looked onto the Barrens for sign of the riders.

Nothing.

Nothing but the sway and dip and cuts of grim surface, spattered grimy mixtures of black, gray, white, and vomit-green where tufts of grass and moss clung to life or where heather clutched hillside. This land, just short of the forbidding landscape of the Black Circle, held rocky juts, and ragged pits milky with mist.

Causing this desolate spillage, in the distance lay the Black Land itself, its ramparts fenced by fanglike mountains. Clouds rolled eternally over the brim of these blasted mountains speaking thunder-belches that quivered the ground from time to time. Winged creatures wheeled over the summits now like ash above a plague fire. Fitful wind blew here, dank and rotten, laced with a briny tang.

Ian left the shelter of the wood for a trail like a jagged fissure, full of cracks for hiding. As his boots hit stone, he swerved. Night hung back among the creepers at the edge of the forest. "Well then, black coward! Going to stay? No curiosity? All right, but don't come to me for dinner scraps no more!"

The dog whined anxiously, then slunk back

among the trees. Ian spat, shrugged, then limped farther along the path, aiming for a higher level and a better view.

The way jerked up, becoming a sloping ledge above a bog streaked with fog. Ian Farthing had nearly attained an abrupt bend of this shelf when the caped woman astride a chestnut mare galloped around the corner, directly toward him.

Here the trail was two yards wide, steeply angled. The horse's eyes were wide and bloodshot and crazed; foam flecked its exposed clenched teeth. The rider's lash snapped the beast's backside frantically. Golden hair escaped a scarf as the woman looked behind her. Terror and desperation marred what Ian could see of her beautiful features.

Ian yelped. He threw his arms protectively about his head. The horse saw him and attempted to avoid him. The woman turned and, seeing Ian, twisted on the leather reins to avoid collision. Her confused mount screeched, leaped, batted the air with front hooves. The stop tossed the woman from her jeweled saddle in a swirl of petticoats. Her horse neighed, its hooves hitting the edge. Loose rocks gave way, propelling the animal down the drop headfirst into the bog. Squirming body; kicking back hooves; twitching tail: then the muck had swallowed the creature up. The stunned woman, sprawled upon the precipitous rock, watched horrified.

Ian took his hands from his head and stared down at the lovely woman. "I don't know what

to say. You should have been watching where
you were headed."

"Crackers!" the young woman screamed, eyes
still fixed on the mottled bog that was her
horse's sticky grave. "Oh, Lord, they'll get me
now. But the runes said I'd get away! Oh dear."
She glared at Ian. "Who are you?"

"Ian Farthing, at your service, m'lady," he
proclaimed humbly, leaning over to assist.

"What? I can't understand what you're saying."

"I'm sorry, but my speech is not the best."
He pulled her up and lamely tried to brush the
dust from her silk dress, full of pink and blue
bows, flounces, and complicated tucks of satin
and silk. It did not look like a riding dress.

"I still can't understand what you're saying,
but we don't have time to talk anyway. Is there
a settlement nearby? A castle at which I might
seek shelter? We must get there quickly. Mullshire, I believe." She breathed hard. Her round
breasts heaved, stretching the lace bodice most
marvelously. Fantasy embodied, this; a fever
dream fleshed out. Absolute mythic perfection.
Ian had never before seen a mouth like that—a
pout, elegant red, stylized faultlessness of curve.
Nor had he seen such a pert nose, nor eyes of
such measureless depth. "We must run! The
Norx are only a short way behind!" She tugged
him on, then proceeded to dash. "You must be
the hero my runes foretold. Is your name
Godfrey?"

No, it wasn't, but Ian grasped his stick hard

and sprinted to catch up. She must be the rider ahead of the other party. And the other three riders must be the Norx, whoever they were. . . .

And who was this woman?

As best he could, he asked.

"Save your breath—we've got to run!" was the answer.

She was as fleet as she was beautiful; before long she had put yards between herself and Ian's limping run. They dashed through the scarred landscape, past outcrops of sandstone and shale, over ledges, down steep leaps to mucky ground. Ian strained to keep pace, wondering what pursued. What manner of creatures straddled those horses he had viewed in the distance?

The woman now seemed merely swirling skirts and lashing lengths of hair as she made for the shelter of the wood.

A steady clop of hooves on stone erupted from behind Ian like thunder from clouds collected unnoticed overhead. Even as he leaned forward to renew his run, he spared a glance over his twisted shoulder. What he saw seemed to slip paralyzing poison into his muscles.

Thirty yards behind, from rocky jaws, the very earth seemed to yawn, spewing destructive specters from the halls of Hell.

The three grew from dusky steeds like monstrous cancers clothed in human finery. Unnaturally long and glistening gray capes flapped and snapped in animate billows as the horrors forged ahead, the winds of passage whistling through the complicated curving of silver swords hilted in finely wrought iron. Their bodies were barrel-shaped, aswarm with knobs and protrusions beneath chainmail. Their legs were short, but their hairy arms were disproportionately long. Gigantic muscles tensed beneath swarthy skin like redwood roots covered by a patina of dirt. As they neared, Ian could discern features on the pumpkin skulls: broad, flat nose; dull, wide-set eyes; a set of walruslike tusks that fitted neatly down chin grooves. Ian had seen more expression on dead men. They emitted no sounds, simply rode, swords raised to clouded sky like lightning rods questing for the sorcerous power of the elements.

"In God's name, help!" cried the woman, still running beyond him, still short of the wood. "They must not catch me or all is lost! Make a stand! They cannot pass a human challenge!"

Abruptly, Ian was aware that he still gripped his staff. He held it before him, grimly facing the closing riders. It felt as though some porcupine of fear grew in his abdomen, bristling its quills of terror.

The rhythm of the galloping horses, the windsounds flicking through the riders' natty apparel, the hiss of the swords wounding the air, created a death dirge that Ian had never before heard, yet somehow recognized. His thoughts fled past fear into panic as the creatures swooped toward him; he was suddenly aware of a warm wetness soaking his crotch, running down his legs.

He had pissed himself.

The humiliating sensation triggered further reaction. His extremities seemed to numb, and, curiously, he grew detached, as though he were floating away from all this. Nothing was terribly important. The staff dropped from his fingers. He turned to one side and walked slowly away from the creatures' path, as though some deep part of him had taken power—an instinct to survive. He didn't know what it was, he simply found himself fleeing.

Then the fit hit.

It wrenched him back to full awareness. Pain crueler than any sword cut from groin to cranium. His arms spasmed uncontrollably, and the sky swirled darkly, giving way to the sight of mud and the scent of grass as the ground slapped his head like a sopping towel. He lay in the muck, twitching uncontrollably, breathing in hoarse and phlegmy spurts.

Vaguely, he became aware of the riders passing in a whirl of legs and swords. An overwhelming stench swooped in their wake; rotting flesh, reeking of cheap perfume.

Ian gagged, then vomited. Suddenly he found himself in possession of his faculties. Wiping his mouth, he blinked and tried to remember what was happening. Sometimes, when he was bored at home, he hyperventilated, then held his breath. The ethereal, unconcerned return from the flirtation with nothingness to waking was the goal, and a momentary loss of memory amid the detached relaxation always accompa-

nied the other sensations. It was like that now
as he lay in the long grass and the mud.

Then he heard the scream.

The musical quality of the cry rendered it all
the more poignant; it rang high-pitched with
the depth of dashed hope and encroaching
despair, soaring through octaves of such con-
summate sadness mingled with wordless terror
that Ian felt his soul yearn to seep from his
frame and blend with this beautiful melancholy,
die with its swan-song passing and so aspire to
oblivion, sweet and soft.

Damn!

Ian yearned to snatch Fate's weaving thread,
yank back the past moments that he might plant
himself firmly in the monsters' path and so, if
the woman was to be believed, halt their forward movement the necessary time for the lady
to escape into the wood.

He had killed her hopes. He knew he was
physically vexed. He thought himself a fool.
Was he an arrant coward as well?

Ian slogged dejectedly to his feet and made
for safer ground. However, even as he began
his trudge, the hellthings broke from the wood,
one bearing the body of the quarry.

The girl kicked and cursed like a dungkeep.

The horses fairly pranced, their fearsome
countenances almost smug. The Norx themselves remained expressionless as ever, two
flanking the one carrying the girl.

Wordlessly, Ian found himself drifting toward
the trooping creatures. The lady ceased her strug-

gle and raised her blond head to spear Ian with a heated stare. "Thanks a whole blessed shitpile of a lot, asshole. You ditch poor Crackers in a sinkhole, then let these turkeys pass you. All you had to do was to say 'Halt!' and put up a bit of a tussle and I could have had a chance. Do you know what you've done? Have you any idea who I am?"

Ian sank to his knees, head bowed in repentance. "What must I do to gain your forgiveness and your freedom, dear lady?"

"What? I can't understand you."

Ian concentrated on a single word. "Do?"

"What can you do? Not a whole lot right now, boyo. You've had your shot. But if you send for some help, that might be nice. Preferably some flashy knights on white chargers rather than the likes of you. It's pretty important. My name is Alandra. If Morgsteen gets me back, before long he'll control the whole Chaos-Web of the Circle!"

The central rider's head jerked toward Ian. Slowly it raised a long, clawlike finger toward him. "Brother Murklung!" The deep sonorous voice issued from its mouth like verbalized putrescence. "Hack!"

chapter three

Ian Farthing's philosophy toward death was similar to that of most mortals: Postpone it at all costs.

So when one of the Norx obeyed its leader's order by drawing its sword and digging spurs into its horse's sides, Ian's first thought was for survival; he began to limp away.

"Oh well," said the captive girl bitterly as the other horses turned and cantered in the opposite direction. "So much for that idea."

Somehow, Ian almost made it to the wood before the Norx caught up.

A steely sigh sounded. The sword scythed down as the rider passed. Ian, hearing this banshee warning, somehow managed to twist away. Only the sword tip touched, ripping his tunic, scratching his upper arm.

It felt like the touch of a torch.

He cried out and fell into glistening loam. The monster's reek enveloped all thought. Ian lay gasping as the thing swerved its beast about and lined up for another go.

This close, Ian could see the Norx clearly. Its face seemed that of a festering corpse, studded with oozy pustules, shiny with a mucousy film. Dead eyes glowed only faintly behind milky curtains. A yolky bristle girded dewlaps.

With a silence deadlier than any warcry, its mouth parted to reveal pointed, corroded teeth. It raised its contorted sword with a green hand and jammed its heels into the stallion's flanks.

Ian squirmed away, whimpering. Weapon held high for the final cut, the rider loomed almost on top of him.

A black snarling streak sailed along the ground and bounced up, colliding with the Norx in a confused flurry of gnashing teeth, gashing claws. The impact toppled the Norx to the ground. Startled, the steed raced away riderless to rejoin its fellows.

Groggily, Ian regained his feet. In the tangle of arms and legs, paws and claws, was a familiar creature, worrying the struggling Norx's neck.

"Night!" Ian cried even as he turned for flight. "Come! Get away!" Night was no match for the Norx, and, weaponless, Ian would be of no help to Night. He stumbled toward the forest. Night's answering bark followed him. As the wood neared, Ian slowed and turned to urge the dog to hurry.

Night had wrested away from the beast, and was about to dash. The Norx grabbed its bushy tail. Night yeaked with pain.

"No!" Ian cried, aghast as Night's doomed eyes looked at him; as the Norx's sword arced down, cleaving the dog in two. A spray of blood swept through the air, spattered the ground. Ian winced, feeling the pain as well.

Grunting with satisfaction, the Norx arose, fishy eyes searching for Ian.

Survival once more sang its song.

For all his grief, Ian flung himself into the forest, lurching desperately across glades and gullies. Soon the Norx was bashing away behind him through bramble and branch. Its speed was amazing for being so heavy. Thump, click, pad, creak; it neared.

The wind soughed around Ian in his stumble-run. His muscles hurt so they seemed to rip from his bones. There was no hope of escaping this behemoth on foot. A few more rods and his legs would give way and the thing would be upon the exhausted remains of Ian's flight, to skewer and slice at its own speed.

No, there had to be another way.

Ian skirted a bower, running around a marshy area foul with bog gas, draped with kudzu. Just as he thought he would have to stop and hide or his legs would turn to jelly, he saw the tree.

A sturdy oak, its leaves were pastelled a deep shade of summer's green, stirring in the fitful Barrens breeze. Its knotty roots peeped up on the edge of a flat area fringed with weeds.

Ian had always been a good climber; he raced for the tree, hoping the Norx was an awful one.

Just at the base of the oak, his foot slipped into the strangely flat ground, not stopping at the surface.

Quagmire!

Fortunately Ian regained his balance. He heaved his boot up with a sucking sound. With a leap worthy of a feline, he grabbed the first tree branch. One hand on raspy bark; two. A heave, an "umph!"; yet still he hung, dangling against the tree side.

The hunter's sounds neared, solemn as the knell of a doom bell and, it seemed to Ian, far more resonant. They inspired him to greater effort. He pulled himself up, snagged a leg over the branch, and swung himself up with surprising agility.

The Norx's sword, bright red with Night's blood, whistled and bit into tree bark, just inches below his hanging leg.

Ian scrabbled to another branch, then another, moving through the woodsy latticework. Twenty feet up, he looked down.

The Norx's face, a study in the grotesque, stared up as expressionless as ever. The thing just stood there, sword ready, glaring at Ian.

With a sudden jump, it reached for the first branch. It's clawlike hand clenched the branch . . . which snapped like a toothpick beneath its ponderous weight.

The Norx slid to the ground, a belchlike "oof!" growling from its throat. It inspected the branch with its hand and flung it away, almost contemptuously.

Ian felt elated. The Norx would be unable to climb the tree! It could not linger. Could it do else but return to its fellows? Whatever magic it owned had no effect here, so that could not be employed against Ian's haven.

He sighed with something like relief, but watched the thing steadily nonetheless.

The monster did an astonishing thing. It hugged the base of the oak.

What? Was it going to try to shinny up? With its weight? That was almost amusing.

But it did not attempt to move up the tree.

It attempted to move the tree.

And it did.

With a creak, the oak shook. Astounded, Ian was almost hurled from his perch. He clamped an arm about the trunk just in time, then flung the other around a nearby branch. Ian clung for dear life. The tree began to sway and shake back and forth. Ian thought he would be unsettled if this madness continued much longer.

Ian's heart seemed to expand to fill this throat. His legs, nearly asleep before in his cramped position, suddenly flared with a fiery iciness. The bumps on the back of his neck seemed to pulse with his dread. The thin wound on his arm seeped blood, stinging mightily.

Then the rocking stopped.

Ian ventured a look downward. The Norx still held the tree, but its breathing was ragged. Had it exerted itself to the full? Hopefully, Ian tilted his head out just enough to gain a better view of the brute.

He went numb.

The tree's trunk—two feet in diameter at least—was cracked. What kind of being was this, to own such power? It was downing the oak by muscle power alone!.

Ian whimpered.

This was it! No hope then. He was for it. That it might take more time made his fate all the more sickening. To be helpless, waiting here to be brought down by the monster, and then dispatched at its leisure . . . awful!

Ian prayed to the God he despised, imploring, promising. He screwed his eyes closed tight, as though to shut out reality. The foul odor of the thing in his nostrils, Ian could almost feel its touch, rough on his neck, hear the snick of the hungry sword.

The tree shook again, shrieking with torn wood. Ian grew faint. A blackness overwhelmed him. . . .

The light-freckled darkness beneath his legs exploded into dazzle.

Contorting light shook, fizzled, took form.

A young man stood before him. A sable coat with an ermine collar hung from broad, manly shoulders. A wave of clean blond hair shook as the handsome fellow frowned.

"Oh, come on, Ian. You know there's only one thing to do," a voice whispered in his ear. A familiar voice!

And Ian had seen the young man, straight and tall, strong and sure, in the mirrors of his dreams.

The vision faded.

"No! No! Come back!" he called. The tree shook more violently, canting. Startled back into cold reality, Ian peered down at the Norx, still intent on its task.

Yes. There was only one thing to do. Somehow Ian knew what that was, now. Better to break his neck going out fighting than to depart this vale of tears whimpering and running, a coward.

He realized, with some astonishment, that he did have a certain kind of courage, and courage born of desperation was better than none at all.

Aiming, he wailed a piercing cry and jumped —feet first.

With a feeling of weightlessness, he plummeted straight down. The Norx, surprised by the shrill scream, looked up, It caught two boots directly in the face. Its nose crunched in. Greenish-red blood oozed as the thing staggered back and back, off balance.

Ian, his fall broken by impact with the Norx, landed in a clump of moss and weeds. Breath partly knocked from him, he nevertheless struggled to his feet to again run.

He saw the Norx staggering back, face smashed, blinded by blood. He saw where it tottered.

Almost over the quagmire!

Not even sparing time to think, Ian sprinted . . . directly toward the Norx.

Leaping up, he struck it on its chainmailed chest, lending its swaying reel just enough direction that it fell back directly into the mire pool. The Norx flopped well toward the center, up to its waist, slobbering and bellowing fiercely.

Ian picked himself up from the ground, watching.

The Norx seemed to recover its senses enough to realize its situation. Slowly, it sank into the stuff. It tried to waddle, wade, or swim back, but each movement dragged it deeper into the quagmire, weighted down as it was by its armor.

Then it ceased thrashing. It stilled, slowly slipping to its death, regarding Ian balefully with catfish stare.

Fascinated, Ian watched, feeling safe.

When the mire was up to its throat, the eyes blazed with something like recognition. The thing spoke in a voice that thundered mournfully. "Had I but known," it ground hoarsely. "I have thrown my present life away. But take my curse." Before it could utter more, its mouth was full of mire. Instinctive struggle simply served to submerge the big head faster.

Confused, Ian picked up the sword that was all that remained of the Norx's visit to the Barrens. Perhaps more of a scimitar than a sword, he noted. Its silvery blade bore some kind of etched runes in the metal. The hilt was crusted over with various jewels—opals, emeralds, sapphires—arrayed in odd patterns.

Recovering his breath and will, he stood by the bog, began to laugh, chortle, snigger.

He had won! For once, he had won!

"Bleedin' scoom face!" he yelled at the mire. "Thought ye had me, didn't you? Well, let me tell you, you had that coming for killing Night. Thought I was a coward, eh? Just because I didn't stand in front of you and your cronies. Let me tell you, I would have, I just . . ."

A hand ripped up through the mottled surface, grabbing a root.

Hardly thinking, Ian raised the blade and chopped. The hand severed at the wrist. The mire top bubbled violently. The bloody arm slithered back into the muck. The separated hand tumbled over onto dry land, into the nook formed by two intersecting roots.

Ian decided it was best to linger no longer in this place.

chapter four

As they crossed the border separating Normality and Magicality, Solid Country from Chaotic Land, Mullshire Province from the Dark Circle, Alandra of Moxmorn thought she would expire with despair.

It was like being dragged into a nightmare, and discovering that nightmare was more real than any waking experience. A clammy wind swirled about her as she bounced painfully before the stolid Norx. The air here seemed charged with uncontrolled energy. Like static electricity, it prickled her hair, shuddered down her backbone, did lunatic dances over the gamut of her emotions.

Was it any wonder she could no longer bear living in such atmosphere? Could she be faulted for escaping toward a saner existence mode? Morgsteen had stolen her from her land and had killed her father, then proclaimed that he loved her and took her to be his bride. Who could have thought that so much importance rested on this delicate body?

The Key, Morgsteen had told her later in his eerie citadel. She was the Key, and . . .

Hooves thundered. A galloping horse approached. She glimpsed it by twisting up her head. It was the beast of the Norx sent to slay that bumbling twit who had fuddled her plans.

The horse was riderless.

Hope filled her. Was it possible that. . . ?

With a fluid motion, the Norx who held her drew rein with his free hand, then barked a rumbling order to the other. His breath slid down upon her like reeking rot. God! Morgsteen would pay for sending such as these . . . if only in the little ways a woman could dish out.

The Norx examined the horse with chilled eyes and grunted. "Of this I was afraid."

"What?" The other grabbed hold of the beast by its mane. "Afraid, Brother Tombheart? Of what?"

"The twisted human. He is more than he seems. I thought I recognized . . . but no. Impossible! Murklung will catch up, Toothmaw. Murklung will catch up. But we must make speed back to the gate."

"Pardon!" shouted Alandra. "Hey! Remember me down here? Your captive?"

"Humble apologies, oh queen," the Norx above intoned. "What is it you wish?"

"That horse there. As long as Murklung isn't in the saddle, why should I not be? It would be much more comfortable and I daresay that Morgsteen would want me comfortable for the journey back. After all, I am his pride and joy."

"Morgsteen, our lord, long may he be Tyrant Glorious of the Nether Realm's Tertiary Quadrant, instructed us to make you most uncomfortable, mistress. He is most distressed at your abrupt departure. Most distressed."

"He's as fickle as a pickle, Tombheart. You know that. With me safely back in his arms, he'll be horrified at the way you've treated me and you'll get privy duty for a week, both of you!"

"But lady," said Toothmaw, "if we put you on the horse, you will surely seek escape again."

"Quite true!" said Alandra disgustedly. "But surely not if you truss me up and hold the reins! Have you no invention?"

A gargling sound: the rare spurt of Norx laughter, from Toothmaw. "Oh, queen, I believe Tombheart enjoys holding you so atop his saddle."

"Silence, infidel! I will brook no further blasphemy," Tombheart roared. "The queen of our lord is as sacred as his royal feces."

"Thanks a bunch for the compliment," Alandra said bitterly.

"Very well," muttered the creature. "You shall have your wish."

He found a leather belt and a long strap, which he tied about her waist. He set her atop the steed and gripped its reins.

They journeyed farther into the quivering atmosphere.

It was a sooty land, a land of mountains and volcanoes, of thunderheads and lightning, of

unsureness and uncertainty. Not barren, but neither full of healthy life. Twisted trees abounded.
Stunted grass, warped flowers. And yet a strangely exhilarating aura charged this land. Magic
hung in the air, thick as mist.

They retraced almost the exact path of her
escape into valleys and up craggy slopes toward
the Portal she had picked. This stood upon
a flat-topped hill not far from the circum-
ferential border.

The Norx slumped into their usual grumbly
silence until, at the base of the slope which led
to the Portal, Tombheart muttered: "I like it
not. Toothmaw, what say you?"

"I do feel an uneasiness in the Fabric, brother.
Things are not right."

"We should restore her highness to Morgsteen
with dispatch. Without her, his control is less."

They galloped up the hill.

And so back into dear Morgy's sweet clutches
to endure his cooing words of endearment,
thought Alandra. Only now he knew he would
have to keep a better watch on his queen. And
now her hope of escape from her hellish existence was practically nil. . . .

They gained the hilltop, and Toothmaw
gasped.

The Portal, once a doorway sculpted of solid
diamond, lay in a tumble of glittering rubble,
sparkling dust.

Tombheart nodded his great head slowly.
"Something is wrong," he said in an awed
whisper. "Something is very wrong."

chapter five

In his enchanted halls, the magus stormed.

"Alabaster!" he cried, stomping from solar to dressing room, from bedchamber to cupola. "Cat! Come to me, immediately!"

His burned arm, dressed in fairy-wing gauze and fragrant with unguents, hung in a sling. His singed hair frizzled. He cursed and he fumed as he climbed the creaking stairway to the last possible hiding place of the sinful feline—the attic. The peeling maroon wallpaper in the section, speckled with fleurs-de-lis, also held a number of Turner landscapes.

The picture frames began to rattle.

The magus halted, taken aback.

So. The unwinding had already begun. It would be necessary to banish the perpetrator of the cosmic gaffe immediately so that the fabric of the Uni-reality centered in the Destiny Game could be painstakingly mended. The wizard hated to dispose of his beloved Alabaster, but the negative vibrations that the familiar had assumed by fouling the dice throw could not be tolerated anywhere in the web-nexus of this vicinity. This could be accomplished by the creature's destruction, but the man would have none of that. Alabaster would simply have to be exiled.

Choking dust spumed from wall cracks. The stairs shuddered. The mansion's very foundation seemed to jerk out of synchrony with this cause/effect plane, wrenching the magus's stomach. He gripped the coiled railing until the tremor passed, then forced his shaken frame to the staircase top.

The rotted door there stood ajar. Alabaster was inside then. Yes. The magus could see paw tracks in the dust. Swinging the door open, he entered, weaving slightly at the loss of balance the negative vibrations of the cat radiated.

"Alabaster," he said in a gentled tone. "I'm not going to hurt you, my dear. Come and be petted. Alabassssster! Sweet kitty!"

He made the ridiculous noises that the cat seemed to respond to, but there was no reaction. The attic was filled with junk draped with dropclothes. Black bunting served as curtain to the single window in the triangularly sloped room. The musky air was wrapped in shadow. The beast could be in any of a number of hiding places, and there was no time to explore them all. He would have to resort to an obedience spell. Tracing complicated signs in the air, the magus crooned a gobbledygook of Latin, Greek, Lemurian, and other obscure languages, punctuating his pronouncement by spitting on the floor. "Well, cat. This means you," he cried even as the rafters shook again with the unraveling threads of the Fabric.

Tail drooped between rear legs, Alabaster emerged from beneath a covered table. "Wasn't my fault, honest!" he said, twitching whiskers. Alabaster seldom used his faculty of human speech; evidently he counted the occasion as an emergency. As well he might. "I don't know what came over me; some sort of magic, for sure, Crowley Nilrem."

"A likely story, beast! You were chasing the ghost mice again, a habit I've warned you against time after time!"

"No, really! That mouse was different! It somehow pulled me after it! I can't explain. My faculties were befuddled. One moment I saw the thing; the next, all was chaos, and you were cursing over your wrecked board, and smoking all over. Do you think a faithful familiar, a courteous cat such as myself, would cause you, whom I love, premeditated harm? Why, pluck out my whiskers and gouge out my eyes and castrate my sex; I'd still be faithful to you, great magus."

The cat bristled with indignity.

Crowley Nilrem, the magus, considered.

Could this be so? Not a trick of fate, not an accident, but a planned attack upon his designs from forces without? But the other Players situated on the various other levels would never stoop to such tactics. They never had before; why should they now? It simply was not how these Destiny Games were played—not at all. A little chaos here and there, certainly. But nothing of this calamitous magnitude.

"Please forgive me, dear kitty. I believe you."

Overjoyed, Alabaster leaped gracefully into the magus's arms, and purred, snuggling against tweed.

"But I'm afraid that I have to do this anyway," the magus continued.

The cat lifted its head, halting its tiny motor-like sound. "Do what?"

"You'll find out, Alabaster," said the magus, stroking the golden fur comfortingly. "Perhaps it will be all for the best. You might be able to help me where you're going, dear estranged familiar."

The cat shrieked and tried to jump from the magus's arms. "Let me go, dammit. I don't wanna go anywhere!" But the magus held fast, and Alabaster was trapped.

"Sshh, sssh, lovely one. Silence. You may return. By the time you return, though, things will have been restored to harmony. Your presence now is devastating. Believe me, if there were any way that I could retain you, I would. But can't you feel the tremors you've caused. You must be hurled away from this continuum."

"Hurled? No!" the cat screamed, clawing at the waistcoat and shirt. "Lemme go. Let me go!" It squirmed frantically, kicking and pushing.

Sorrowfully, the magus clutched harder and descended the staircase, crossed the dining room, descended another coiling set of stairs, then navigated the stone steps to his workroom, where the necessary Portal could be conjured. All the while, he spoke to the cat in soft tones, assuring it that this was the only measure short of death he could take to preserve the rapidly disintegrating Continuity of the mansion. The plaster of the walls was cracking. The jeweled chandeliers jingled and the bulky furniture jumped. Tables toppled and loose things—bric-a-brac, pictures, books—bumped one after another to the carpet.

Back in his chamber of legerdemain, the magus hurried to a walnut cabinet. The lab equipment on his worktable tinkled. Phials and test tubes burst, their contents spraying. The magus pulled the cabinet's zinc handle and uttered spell words, achieving immediate effect.

The glossy wood of the interior dissolved to a boiling mist, which dissipated to present an unhindered view of a cosmos shaft. Stars and gases twinkled and twirled in a primped velvet emptiness. The sight presented the impression of limitless extent, bottomless depth.

Leaning through this aperture, Crowley Nilrem peered about.

Downward, to the left relative to the position of this perforation into the sorcerous other side of the Uni-reality: There is was! A swirling of clouds, like a hurricane viewed from above: the Maelstrom. The Dark Land. The Black Circle. To toss Alabaster randomly through the Portal might mean he would drift for ages before lighting upon solid material. But a throw toward the Maelstrom, the central vertex of the forces of Chaos, would speed the process. The cat would land in a place where, after suitable exile, it could find the series of gates back to this level.

The magus craned his familar through the hole, aiming the sobbing cat for the circular formation. "Dear Alabaster, believe me. This pains me more than you can know. But we will meet again before you know it."

"You'd better believe it, Nilrem! Then it will be my turn to kick your ass out here and . . ."

The magus smiled kindly. With compassion, he flung the beast. Alabaster dropped quickly, head over paws in mad, twirling, screeching outrage. Down and down, through the star-specked black washed in random painter's palettes of color and delineating threads of the reality levels, the tiny beast tumbled . . . till it was no more than a fleck of gold reflecting the starglow; and finally, nothing at all.

Crowley Nilrem sighed deeply and stepped back from the opening, intoning the words for the rematerialization of the cabinet. This complete, he shut the doors and turned to see about returning equilibrium to his home.

First, it was necessary to restore order to the playing pieces upon the Destiny Board.

The magic hall smelled of spilled elixirs and oils. A smog of gases curled from the worktable above smashed glass. But propelling the entropy-focus, poor innocent Alabaster, away from this plane seemed to have helped. Nothing shook now, at least—though that did not mean that things had been righted in the main. Nilrem walked to the table, picked up his chair, and sat, leaning close for contemplation, trying to reconstruct the previous formation of pieces.

The characters were standing again.

The magus stared at the board, shocked. The playing pieces, once scattered and fallen, were upright once more—and in markedly different positions! How could this have happened? Impossible!

Nilrem studied the new patterns. He looked to the playing area where the fall of the magic dice would have made their main impact. As he suspected, Queen Alandra's piece was flanked by Norx pieces. Strange . . . only two of them! Even so, this certain and uncompromising capture would be hard to nullify after all the work it had taken to transfer her from Morgsteen's Citadel through the hyper-portal. It would take much more effort to wrest her away from Morgsteen again. Much willpower, much concentration. Perhaps a brief alliance with Trilawnie the Mirthful would consolidate sufficient power to influence compensation for this unexpected occurrence. . . .

His musings were suddenly interrupted as his eyes wandered over something even more astonishing.

A short distance from the scene of reapprehension on the board, there stood a new piece.

It seemed the representation of a man—but it was hard to say, so poorly was it constructed.

The piece consisted of plywood scraps, thumb-tacks, and paper clips. It head was a tin thimble, painted with yellow dots for eyes, a round dab of blue for a nose, and a ludicrously curved line of purple for a smiling mouth. The wood body was markedly bent. One foot appeared mangled. It stood facing the square marked Mullshire, stiff doll hands awkwardly outstretched.

In one of those hands was a Norx sword.

The magus leaned closer to inspect it further, immediately drawing back, nose twitching with disgust.

It smelled awful.

Playing pieces didn't give off odors. What was this?

But before he could contemplate the matter further, his attention was distracted to the opposite side of the circle to a square partly in the gray area, partly overlapping the Magic Circle's black, marked with a particularly complex manse/fortress piece. Adjacent to the square, firmly planted in the gray, was a flying war machine, directed toward a circuitous route around the Dark Circle. Beside the flying machine was the frightful sculpture of Roth Kogar.

Crowley Nilrem blanched. His mouth grew dry, and his breathing became sporadic. Irler Mothwing had chained the dreaful despot to his castle turns ago. How could he have escaped, and with a flying machine? Things were far worse that Nilrem had imagined, for there was only one place that Roth Kogar, drinker of blood, tantamount tyrant, slayer of children, could be headed, and that destination portended grim events to come:

Mullshire.

chapter six

For Ian Farthing the league journey back to Mullshire consisted of breathless spurts of running, several limping walks to catch that lost breath, and more than one tumble to the grass to summon more strength.

He had buried the Norx sword amid a copse of trees, marked by a large rock for easy finding. If Ian Farthing the idiot sauntered into town bearing a blade like that, chances were the knights would trust him only after they'd pincushioned him with arrows. It would have been a nice bit of proof; but it was readily available if it was needed.

He almost preferred the pain of the run to the agony of memory that caught him when at rest.

Night. Jolly, happy Night. The dear dog was dead now. Hadn't the faithful creature warned him not to walk out on the Barrens? If only he had listened ... so much would have been different. The woman would have galloped to the protection of Mullshire castle. Night would not have had to surrender his life.

Things, however, could not be changed. All he could hope was that he could convince some knights to follow the Norx and their captive. The woman might yet be saved.

But he must hurry. . . .

So he strained for all he was worth, keeping the image of the beautiful damsel alive in his mind.

Before long he topped the last grassy knoll. The sight of the town, the castle, and much of the manor of Mullshire awaited him.

Mullshire Castle was the center, with its four high, red-flagged towers, its forty-foot gray stone curtain walls, its lilypad-and-weed-clogged moat . . . its colored banners on poles above the gatehouse and the barbican opposite the drawbridge. The Druid River slipped to one side of the castle. Boats and skiffs cruised here, merchant vessels no doubt traveling to or from Dirkwood or Lassington or Talltower . . . all within the greater kingdom of Harleigh.

Across the river lay thatched farm sheds, neatly patterned fields studded with workers. The concentration of Mullshire activity, though, both urban and agrarian, lay this side of the Druid. The city itself seemed an outgrowth of the imposing castle. This urban area consisted of a honeycomb of sometimes cobbled, more often dirt roads, lined with houses.

Among these streets Ian had lived and grown from the age of six. His "parents" were only his wards. He had been found, a wandering urchin, by a cobbler's wife with no children of her own. She had convinced her dour husband, with much bullying and an occasional soulful smack, that this orphan should be housed under their roof and treated as their natural son. Ian had no memory of this. However he did have one odd recollection: waking up near the moors at the Dark Circle's verge, clothed only in tattered rags and without the faintest idea of who he was or where he had come from. Mostly what he remembered was how cold it had been; all shivers and shakes, quivers and quakes. He did not remember how he had survived the windy moor, nor how he had discovered the town of Mullshire.

The fact that he was not blood kin to Soames Farthing and his bloated wife Matilda was not revealed until one night some ten years before, when his father had drunk too much ale and tried to beat him, calling him a no good gutter-bastard. Cat out of the bag, Matilda Farthing had explained the entire story to Ian. Of the community, she was one of the two people not disgusted with his appearance, the other person being Hillary Muffin.

Ian loved his mum for that, if for nothing else. Still, there was much more to love. Without her and Hillary and the occasional gruff and dearly bought sign of affection from the old cobbler, life would simply be unlivable.

Sometimes he wished he were a villein's son, living out in the near countryside in a simple oblong cottage, tilling the fields, absorbed in nature and a solitary life. Instead he was crushed into the mainstream of things, caught in the worst of circumstances for a disfigured young man considered a simpleton. In the cruel life of the streets he was allowed no respected social position despite his solid skill as a craftsman now taking the bulk of his father's business upon his crooked shoulders.

Normally the Mullshire knights—the military elite who presided over the rabble of serfs and craftsmen that would become an army if protection was needed—could be found within the castle walls. But today was Festival Time—a spring fête, celebrating the grudging arrival of spring after a bitter winter—and the knights would be carousing and making mirth in the streets and inside taverns. It would be in the alehouses and gaming hells, among the crowded stalls and the dark dives, that Ian would find them.

He only prayed that their desire for adventure would outweigh the nature of the message's bearer. He also prayed his story could be understood. His speech impediment could sometimes be overcome if he remained calm and mouthed the words slowly.

Yes, they would have to understand. He would make them understand.

Ian skirted a windmill of ocher wood. The white sails upon the lattice of blades billowed and flapped, pushing the central screw to grind the grain inside. He passed through one of the three main outlying fields of agriculture surrounding the town; the principal arable area

was divided into triple segments planted in
rotation. One year one held wheat, another oats,
and the last remained fallow. In separate gar-
dens beyond and within the actual town boundaries peas, rye, beans, and vetches were culti-
vated. The town's sheep were folded and cattle
herded on these plains in the winter and early
spring for their manure; Ian could see them far
and near.

He hobbled past one of the several plowmen
working despite the holiday. The farmer used a
wooden swing plow tethered to four straining
black-spotted heifers. The middle-aged man
grumbled above the smelly earth, urging his
beast to hurry that he might finish this burden-
some task so he could join the gay festivities,
sounds from which floated over the damp, glistening weeds and upturned soil.

Finally he approached the inauspicious be-
ginnings of Mason Street, its dilapidated hov-
els deserted now, the denizens at the fair. Ian
hurried down the rutted road, turned onto
Ha'penny Trail, moving past grand, many-gabled
houses, freshly whitewashed fences with flowers growing among the green turf fronting them.
A right at Ribbon Way took him past all manner of cottages, huddled closely together, chiefly
reserved for castle servants.

Close to the city's center was Merchants'
Square, a park filled with apple trees around
which shops and stores collected like blossom-
ing fruit. Ian's hurry was soon slowed by the
crush of celebrants spilling into the surround-

ing roads and blocks of congestion. Booths and stands displayed all manner of merchandise from bolts of fine clothes to rare spices, tinkers' ware to leatherwork. Delicious smells twirled on wings of smoke; food was available from harsh-voiced hawkers: meat savories, crisp peach tarts, hot cross buns, charcoal-roasted chestnuts. The crowd churned and rumbled with delight, turned out in their best clothing. Women wore long embroidered cottes; men were in bright surcoats. The throng seemed a seething of hues, pleasant scents, abrupt food aromas in the air, and bumping, pushing arms and muffled bodies good-naturedly jostling from site to site of selling or entertainment.

Exhausted, Ian shoved his way quickly through to the middle. The main alehouse, the Crowing Cock, lay on the other side of the square. Strains of music filled the air; soon Ian saw bands of roving minstrels bowing rebecs, plucking harps, blowing shawns, or strumming gitterns. Bagpipes and coremuses abounded; all manner of cymbals, clappers, and timbrels supplied their separate rhythms to the confused cacophony of the individual lilting or brassy tunes that floated through and above the milling people like aural mist. Jugglers threaded delicately through, tossing bright balls, oranges, lemons, bowling pins high into the air and catching them on their descent, only to hurl them up again toward the clear sunshiny sky. All kinds of games were in progress: draughts, chess, backgammon, blindman's buff, and hot cockles. On each cor-

ner of the square were puppet shows, surrounded by goggling children dressed in a riot
of color. A delirious madness spread like a
palpable joyous sheet over all proceedings. The
infectious air of delight penetrated even Ian's
somber heart. He wished he could stop and
mingle—but he had a duty. He had to get to the
knights, across the way. . . .

He shoved and dodged across the park's trampled grass, ducking under apple-tree branches
and jumping odd obstacles. On the other side,
he found himself impeded by the spectacle
streaming through Bricher's Corner. There was
no way he could slip through the tight-packed
Mullshiremen, staring, fascinated, at the series
of wagons—long, horse-drawn flat carts, each
bearing amateur actors in elaborate costumes
situated in unusual scenes.

Mystery plays.

A long cycle of mystery plays, seemingly
linked in a train that told an entire story.

Because he could not squeeze past, Ian halted.
Having no other choice, he watched.

Evidently, the cycle had just begun. The only
action occurred now upon the foremost cart;
the actors upon the others were frozen in pictur-
esque friezes. This first cart displayed a set of
shiny feather gates. Men with wings, draped in
white flowing robes, stood about in prayerful
attitudes: angels.

Upon a raised wood dais stood a large throne,
its topmost half covered by a ruffled silk curtain.
Legs wrapped in vermilion robes and feet

THE DESTINY DICE 63

adorned with paste-jewel-studded sandals pro-
truded beneath the breeze-whipped curtain. A
man sat on the throne.

The scene, then, would be Heaven. The man
on the throne represented God Himself.

Concealed, God had His forearm thrust through
a parting of the curtains, pointing at the confused collection of struggling angels at the edge
of the wagon. "Dearly beloved Lucifer, keeper
of the music of the spheres, musician of Mine
heart," a voice thundered. "You have conspired
to topple Me from Mine own throne in Heaven
High, to assume rulership of the Universe
yourself. Your pride has puffed you up. You
have turned many of My angels' heads from
the true light to thine darkening self. But the
forces of My archangels Gabriel and Michael
have smited you down, and behold! Now you
grovel, awaiting well-deserved punishment.
What say you before sentence is served and
acted?"

The cluster of angels scattered apart, creating a semicircle of bent-winged, droop-haloed
guards about a single imposing individual, dark
of brow, with a rent, sullied robe. This figure
proceeded to gesture rudely toward the throned
deity, which brought laughter and foot-stomping
from the crowd. "Ho ho, You snot-faced ogre,"
the rebel said. "You villainous coward. So You
have won this round, dear Jehovah, by lulling
me into believing the power I have collected
these eons against you was sufficient. But now
I have a measure of Your might. I shall not rest

until You see that I am Your equal and You have no right to be the tyrant You are. So do Your worst, Jovey, 'cause You're going to get it back, eventually. Doubled."

The powerful, tattered figure of Satan continued his tantrum.

Then suddenly smoke poured from atop the curtains. The cloud-cracking voice boomed again: "You've really gotten Me upset now, Lucifer. Your perverse games have gone too far. Even now, on My new planet Earth, in its very center, I have created a place for your prison term. Hot. Evil. Livid lava. And when I cast you into the lake of fire there—"

"Why not just shorten it to H.E.L.L.—Hell, gracious Jehovah on high? It rhymes with 'bell' and therefore has a lovely ring to it!" suggested an angel by the curtain, holding a bright brass trumpet.

"Hmm. A good name. And so, Lucifer, you will stay in Hell until you mend your prideful ways!" The hand snapped Its fingers. "Kick him out! And the other traitors with him!"

"Better to rule in hell," Lucifer bellowed, "than to arrange Your stupid chorales of praise!"

Even as he spoke these words a little boy—a cherub—bounced out, holding a silver lyre. "Dear choirmaster," piped the pretty, apple-cheeked youngster. "You've forgotten your favorite instrument. We and the seraphim will pray for your release and reinstatement night and day!"

The somber surrounding angels swooped in

upon Lucifer, grabbing him and inadvertently carrying the unfortunate cherub along with the flailing upstart.

The lyre remained, bent, strings broken, on the ground in the scuffle's wake.

Lucifer and his minions, portrayed by three men in ripped robes, were tossed from the platform into the dust, the horrified cherub with them. They rose, brushed themselves off with great dignity, then strode to the next wagon. The cherub sobbed, "But I didn't do anything wrong. Why am I falling with you?"

"Quiet!" shushed the others. "Of course you belong in this fall. God does not make mistakes." Lucifer sauntered at the forefront of this motley collection. He hopped upon the next car, which graphically depicted the tortures and fires of Hell with much red and orange crepe paper and firepots issuing faint smoky wafts of burned, rotten-egg odors.

By now Ian recognized the tale being presented in play form: It was the legend of Laslo, the Cherub Tossed from Heaven by Mistake. Finding him in Hell, Lucifer would have nothing to do with him, calling him a little God-loving wimp and hurling him back to Heaven. But Lucifer's aim was awry and the young angel landed on Earth many years after Adam and Eve had died, and was forced by circumstances to wander, trying to convince humans and God Himself that he was an angel and deserved a place in the Celestial Home.

It was a sad and funny story cycle that Ian

Farthing liked very much; but there was no time to watch this mystery-play version now. As it happened, just as the Hell portion of the tale was finishing, Ian espied both a break in the crowd that would allow him passage and a place to slip between the wagons of the pageant. Rested somewhat, he hobbled through and was just passing one of the wagons when the actor playing Laslo the cherub—a runt-faced midget on his way to the next float—stumbled into him. "God's corns!" cried the man. "Watch where you're going. I've got another scene to do!" The little man hustled away . . . leaving a small, thin object behind in the dust.

Ian scooped this up, bawling after the midget: "Hallo! You dropped . . ." But the little man did not hear and was well into the next scene, so Ian moved down the alleyway that would lead to the Crowing Cock. As he moved he examined the item. A short metal cylinder, it shone as though made of silver. At one end was a tiny hole; on the other was a metal stud. Ian placed his thumb on the stud, accidentally applying pressure. The stud gave way with a click. A tiny pointed rod filled the aperture. Astonished, Ian pressed the stud again. The little rod was pulled back into its hole! Incredible.

On one side of the cylinder, by the clicking stud, was a short clip of metal, open at one end. Remembering his mission, Ian slipped the thing into his pouch and moved down the crooked alley, which reeked with sewage and refuse clogged in stagnant puddles in the drainage gutter.

Above, shutters clacked against stone walls and a woman's voice grated: "Gangway!" A shower of unspeakable slop splattered on stone in front of Ian.

"Bloody hell!" Ian cried, looking up. A cracked chamberpot was being hauled back into a small, pitted window by wrinkled hands. "Watch out where you throw!"

A globule of spittle arched majestically from the window, landing directly on Ian's forehead. "Next time it's on you, gimpy!"

The shutters slammed closed.

Ian wiped the gunk from his face and stepped gingerly through the remainder of the alleyway, alternating careful eyes between ground and high windows.

The alleyway led out upon a congested, highly trafficked street that was not much wider. Bits of the fair were stationed here on Huggers Street, surplus flotsam from the cramped square. Across the cobblestoned way lay the Crowing Cock, an inn of ill repute and much popularity, its sectioned windows all but opaque with condensation and grime. Drunken men stood by the doorway under an elaborate sign emblazoned with a red-and-blue rooster perpetually and silently trumpeting dawn. Others lounged on weathered, creaking benches, watching the crowds mill by, clenching iron mugs as though fearful the vessels of brew might sprout legs and run off.

Ian negotiated the width of the street cautiously, then stopped short of a group of men, obviously knights by the coats of arms that labeled their tunics. They buzzed with vibrant conversation, songs and curses, slapping knees and the backsides of their attendant pitcher-bearing pages with bluff abandon.

Ian chose the nearest—a paunchy, pinch-cheeked man wearing a purple ale-splotched tunic. Ian drew himself up to his full height and said, "Please, your highness, I need help. Out on the barrens I happened on a young woman, fleeing from terrible, fiendish creatures of the Black Circle, and—"

The knight's misty, dark eyes focused and stared down at Ian. "What did you say, boy? Haven't you the courtesy to address me in more fluent speech if you've the gall to address me at all?"

Ian thrust a finger toward the top of his mouth. "I have a speech problem, good knight, which renders my—"

"Get your hand out of your mouth and you might make some sense."

The knight was drunk. He exuded ripe, yeasty breaths far more explicit than the generally stale, aley atmosphere clinging to the inn front. Lifting his hefty flagon, he downed a long gulp, snowing his thick bushy black mustache with foam, which splattered into Ian's face with the man's next words. "D'ye say 'lady,' craven? Lady. You want to sell me your sister?" His locks rocked with his laughter. "Lads! Lads, the buzzard is selling his sister!"

Heads turned.

"What did ye say your name was again?" the knight asked.

"Ian Farthing, sir, a poor cobbler by trade. But about what I was saying, which is of the utmost importance—"

"A farthing!" cried the knight. "She'd better have more looks on her than you, cripple!" He exploded with laughter. The other knights, drifting forward to stick their ears into the confusion, echoed their own cackles and boozy coughs. Old knights, young knights: knights with scars and knights with missing fingers, no nose, or chopped earlobes.

"Please, sir!" Ian cried, frustrated, tears starting warm in his eyes. "You must listen. If you don't come with me, I cannot ever redeem myself of my mistakes! In God's name, listen!" He had become so flustered that his mouth chopped the sounds into verbal sausage, understandable to no one. The knights again bellowed with laughter at this poor red-faced sot clutching and unclutching his hands, tears running down pocked cheeks. It drove Ian into further indecipherable outbursts.

A young man separated himself from the throng. He threw an arm over Ian, displaying a flat palm to halt the noises of the collected audience.

"Please!" he said in a cultured accent. "I know this young fellow and can speak his reputation. Give me but a moment, if you will." The young knight wore a tan cotehardie, with his coat of arms—swords and evergreens—

emblemed on his right breast just before the draping lavender cape, cut at the hem to hang down in long strips. His tight pants were scarlet, his brown leather shoes quite pointed. A long, richly jeweled belt slipped low on his hips, carrying a dagger in a cowhide sheath. Below his dark felt hat, fastened by a rubied brooch, raven's-wing hair curled lavishly, filling out a thin, delicately featured face.

The crowd quieted. Ian looked up at the blue-eyed man with anxious hope. An uneasy memory formed at the back of Ian's mind . . . one that he could not quite totally grasp.

"Ah yes! Thank you," said the man smoothly. "Thank you, indeed. Now, as I was saying . . . our young friend's reputation . . . and perhaps an explanation of his presence today."

"The lady . . . please, let me tell my tale!" Ian cried, excited. Perhaps he could form a rescue party after all! "The Barrens! They're taking her away! The Norx! She must be a princess. Beautiful! Please, help me rescue her!"

"My goodness, you don't say!" cried the young knight. "But really, my friend, you must be quiet for just one moment." Thin finger to thinner lips. "A little background on you to these knights who lack understanding. And I must admit, I glean little meaning from your words myself. But . . ." He turned to face the audience, assuming a highly formal and haughty manner. "Gentlemen. May I present, for your approval, Ian Farthing. I have the pleasure of knowing Mr. Farthing for quite some time, although in the past decade Fate has taken us on separate paths."

Know me? thought Ian. But who. . . ?

"Gentlemen, I quite assure you that here, for your express pleasure, is an excellent sportsman. Many a pleasant hour have I spent with this fine fellow, gaming with the lads in Spittle Mews and Dank Alley—when in the interest of a more diverse education I mingled from time to time with the common folk. And here, to my surprise, Ian has presented himself before us all to increase our enjoyment of this fine day of celebration. Please be assured, my friends, that Ian is quite harmless."

"But what the deuce does he do besides burble nonsense?" someone cried.

"What else does he do?" cried the young knight, throwing a forearm over his forehead in mock anguish. "What does this fine, talented, foul-smelling little dungpile dunce do? Why sirrah, behold the finest jester of the kingdom!"

Oh no! thought Ian. Godfrey—

"Make them laugh, clown!" And the young knight deftly tripped Ian with a leg and a well-placed shove.

chapter seven

Godfrey Pinkham!

The name flashed through Ian's mind even as he toppled over, frantically wind-milling for balance, into the filthy street.

"And pleased observe! A most excellent dirt dancer!" announced Sir Godfrey Pinkham, expertly kicking Ian in the midriff. Pain flowered out into a spasm of his muscles, turned into a garbled cry of hurt. Ian rolled on the street, twitching and kicking spasmodically.

Surprised knightly laughter rang in his ears.

"No, please! You must listen to me—!"

"My goodness, what did you say, sportsman?" Godfrey Pinkham leaned over toward the fallen, hand cupped to ear.

"Godfrey—please don't—I must explain—"

"Dear me!" Godfrey cried dramatically. "The jester is so happy by your esteemed response, he says to kick him again, but this time in the arse. Shall I oblige?" He turned to the audience, eyebrows lifted in question.

Much clopping of mugs and flagons ensued,

boosted by cheers and cries of "Yes! Yes!" from those sober enough to speak.

Shuddering, Ian breathed deeply and tried to get up, attaining a hands-and-knees crawling position, attempting to scuttle away like a crab. If only he had known that Godfrey Pinkham would be here! The highborn Godfrey had been the bane of his youth—alternately endearing friend and rough bully. Sometimes Godfrey acted as though he were compassionate and understanding of Ian's problems, apologizing for his roguish behavior . . . and then suddenly turned into a brash bully and shamed Ian before his street-kid peers. Then, when Godfrey had become a page at age eleven, Ian had seen him no more.

"God's blood," said his tormentor. "Behold the marvelous target he presents me! Dear Fart! You haven't changed!"

Ian turned his head just in time to see a flying foot and a nasty leer on Godfrey's face. Then he felt the hard shove of sharp shoe on rear, and was pushed nose first into the dust, which spewed into his nostrils, choking him. He coughed and tried to wipe the grit from his face.

"And so, gentlemen, you see the finest fool of Mullshire in the midst of his performance!" Godfrey said glibly after the laughter and clapping died down. Please note the exquisite melancholy of his method of self-expression. How droll he renders his bon mots! And the skill and litheness of his pratfalls have improved so much since last I observed them!" He patted his hands in gentle mocking applause. "Bravo! Bravo, dear jester! But has the delivery of your jokes improved? Alas, I see that in your enthusiasm you have gotten quite dirty. Allow me to wash your face!" He espied a large pitcher of ale on a nearby table. "Ah ha! What a marvelous basin for the toilette!"

Sniggling with enjoyment, he turned and strode toward the pitcher.

Ian spit dirt from his mouth and opened his eyes, immediately seeing what Godfrey intended. Oh, how he wished he were stronger and could defend himself. Years of bitter frustration choked his throat, and tears streamed down his grime-crusted face. How he would avenge himself! The people would laugh at torturers like Godfrey, not at their victims. Oh, the havoc he would—

Hold a moment, he thought.

That Norx this morning had not been a weak squirrel. And Ian had beaten him for all his lack of coordination. Luck perhaps. Desperation, true, drove him to it. But compared with the Norx, Godfrey was puny.

And he didn't have to kill Godfrey.

Suddenly Ian felt a strange sensation, a power, a lightness. Quickly he jumped to his feet in a crouching stance. And before the crowd could cry warning, he found himself charging the retreating Godfrey Pinkham with a speed and intent that truly surprised him.

Godfrey had just reached the foamy pitcher

when Ian jumped. The wild leap plunged the knight's head through the wide mouth of the pitcher, dunking it into the brew.

The crowd gaped in dumb astonishment as Ian, little less amazed himself, yanked Godfrey Pinkham back to his feet, letting the ale splash and dribble down the front of the man's cape and tunic and pants, thoroughly drenching them with the ripe, rank stuff. Skull stuck inside the empty pitcher, Pinkham spluttered and spat hollowly inside, trying to push the wood container off with both hands, leaving the rest of his body totally unguarded.

Hardly considering what he was doing, Ian promptly kneed the knight in the groin. Godfrey's muted cry was horrendous as his arms and hands abandoned the pitcher to belatedly protect himself. Moaning wretchedly, the knight doubled over.

Ian immediately took advantage of the situation by grasping the stricken Godfrey by both shoulders, darting a quick gaze down the street, then shoving the newly helmeted man hard, backward.

Groaning, the knight plummeted back in a crazy teetering dance for balance, finally losing his footing and squishing on the exact target Ian had espied: a round, wet, stinking pile of fresh horse manure, abuzz with flies.

Ian turned and addressed the shocked audience. "Now! Will you kindly listen?"

A man bellowed, pointed a hand. "Kill the scummy bastard!"

" 'Twas a fair fight!" cried Ian, but the crowd of brawny knights had begun to surge forward, calloused hands outstretched to seize him.

Godfrey Pinkham had just hoisted the pitcher from his dripping head when Ian whizzed past. The wet knight hurled it at Ian, but it fell short. Pinkham, ranting with fury, awkwardly pushed to a stand. He was about to lead the gauntlet of pursuit when the crowd overtook him, bumping him down once more, face first into the dung heap.

Meanwhile, Ian ran with all the speed his aching legs could muster down the market-congested street, banging off wooden stalls, spilling fruit stacks and carts of leather goods, caroming off hawkers and customers alike in his mad dash to escape. The drunken knights, tunics and capuchons in various states of disarray, bumbled after him, crashing into baskets of vegetables, upturning grilles of frying lamb joints and beef strips in their reckless pursuit of the jester who had so ignobly disgraced their brother.

The turmoil added a madcap element to the steady uproar of the Spring Fair. Cages of chickens were sent crashing to the curb, spewing gusts of feathers and outraged bird yawks to the confusion. The jumbled smells and textures of the jammed street seemed to Ian to condense into solid sensation—and then simply fade, giving way to his frantic gulpings for breath, the straining of his spent muscles, and the taste of blood arising from the back of his throat. His run was a forced pell-mell zigzag averting some collisions with obstructions, jumping over others, and simply plowing through most.

Finally, the sight of his goal approached: a narrow slit between two squat buildings. This alley would lead to a complicated series of similar alleys. He leaped through the opening and lunged into its protective, damp shadows. Halfway down this esophagus of darkness, he heard a clamor: the pursuers, pushing themselves through after him. If they apprehended him now, he would be lucky if he got off with broken limbs and no front teeth. He swerved quickly into a perpendicular branch of the alley, splashing through noisome puddles, then turned into another alley covered by planks one story above, rendering it quite dark.

Ian paused to catch his breath, stooping and spitting phlegm from his exertion, feeling nausea worm through him. Hearing the shouts of his pursuers, he straightened and was about to push his agonized body farther when a shaft of light abruptly streamed down from above, fixing him with its sunny brightness.

Shielding his eyes from the light, he peered up fearfully as though he expected God Himself to be the originator of this pillar of light. Framed in the aperture formed by the lifted plank was the silhouette of a head, light catching in a draping of curling red hair.

"Ian!" a soft but insistent voice said. "Ian

Farthing! Quickly. Up here! They're swarming all through the alley maze. Hurry!"

Only one other person called this honeycomb of paths the alley maze. "Hillary?"

"Yes, yes, you lummox. Climb up those barrels there, put your foot on the windowsill, and take my hand!"

Yes ... there were barrels, wooden barrels hooped around by metal, up against the wall. And above: a shut window with sufficient sill to hold a boot. Quickly, Ian leaped atop the closest barrel, hoisted his foot to the ledge, and pushed himself up, reaching for the hand that dangled from the brightness. He caught the wrist, and the hand curled around his own wrist, and he jumped for all he was worth, flailing for purchase on the crevices in the stone. The tip of his boot slipped into a crack, and the hand pulled hard and another hand descended, snatching hold of his collar and yanking. His free hand caught the top of the flat roof, and he pulled and shoved with his planted foot, the hands from above clutching at his shirt, tugging mightily at his belt, helping. He lifted himself over the wall and flopped onto the roof.

"Get your big feet out of the way," said Hillary Muffin, grasping the plank by one end to heave it back into place.

Ian obliged tiredly. The young woman refitted the wood.

"I saw it all, Ian Farthing. You shouldn't have done that to that knight. You should have just run." A smile slid reluctantly onto her lips. "I must say, though, it was worth it, seeing him flounder about with the wooden eyeless heaume atop his noggin!"

She chuckled girlishly.

"Thanks, Hiller." He looked up at her, crouched over him.

Hillary Muffin was the only one besides his mum who tried to understand Ian. Strangely, perhaps she did that best. Fifteen years old, she was a slender thing, barely breasted, with slim hips and long gawky legs. Her hair was an autumn red—a dusky, dark red that seemed to magically shift hues to a sort of dark blond if backlit. She wore it very long and full, to cover as much of what she considered an inadequate face as possible.

"You're just bloody lucky, 'sall I can say. But c'mon. Let's get out of here before they think of checking the roofs." She made a face, wrinkling her nose. "Christ, you smell like an uncleaned privy!"

"Well, dammit, 'tis truth you'd reek too, you'd been through what I been through!"

Hillary put a finger to her lips. "Pipe down, huh? You want to put them onto us?"

"Uhm . . . sorry." Even as he said this, he heard the loud shots and clamor of approaching knights, streaming through the alleyways, bumping into one another in the darkness. No, Hillary was quite right—it wouldn't be long before they realized that he must have somehow gotten up to one of the roofs. How many of them were there in that besotted company? Ian realized he'd had no time to count.

Without another word, Hillary struck out across the the makeshift bridge to the next rooftop. Ian carefully followed, trying to make his footfalls as quiet as possible.

The rooftops of Mull, sprouted with intermittent trees, made a bizarre landscape of chimneys, odd architectural outcrops of smoke, curling black in the breeze. In the distance stood the high spires of Mullshire Cathedral. To the left stood the battlements and towers of Mullshire Castle. Ian followed Hillary for what seemed a long time, keeping to the wood-shingled roofs, avoiding the hazardous thatched sorts. They leaped the chasms between the buildings, crept along precipitous ledges, climbed uncertain slopes of cracked slate shingle. The peculiar paths and angular byways of this level of the town were by no means unfamiliar to him; but today he had some problems negotiating it all with ease because of the unusual exertion he had been forced to expend. Generally, his misshapen limbs gave him no trouble. Today they did, and he almost fell, twice.

Soon they reached an alcove that was their sanctum sanctorum: a cleft in a building with a trellised balcony hanging with luxuriant ivy that completely hid the ignored space beneath. It was here that, smarting with society's wounds or Da's feeble whippings, Ian would retreat when he did not care for the woods beyond the fields. Precious little time was allowed for any sort of retreat; but what he could procure, Ian took and treasured highly.

Hillary crawled through the leafy entrance first. Ian followed. In these cool shadows, high enough to escape the stench that often hugged the ground, the air was scented with the small flowers in boxes siding the balcony. With a sigh of relief, Ian collapsed upon a woolen blanket, feeling truly safe and comfortable at last. Hillary rummaged about in an old trunk, drew something out, and placed it on a shelf that Ian had built himself years ago when he had first realized this place's potential. The ivy halted much of the light, but what seeped through dappled the darkness in a cozy, unthreatening manner. Ian frankly liked it this way—but Hillary would have more light.

With a tinderbox she flicked a spark, nursed it to a small flame, and with this lit a fat old candle formed of the dead wax of candles Ian collected whenever possible. The flame caught and guttered nervously, then slid fully down the wick, licking up a healthy tongue of red-and-yellow light. Hillary snuffed the tinderbox flame, then turned to Ian, freckled face concerned, hair aglow from the candle rays.

"You all right, Ian? You don't look good. You were hopping these roofs like a one-legged toad. What happened today that sent you scurrying to that den of vipers? I've been looking for you all day. Thank God I glimpsed you passing the wagon pageant, or those king's turds would be flogging you yet. How ever did you flummox that pansy-faced one?" All in one long chatter the words gushed, demanding, scolding, and caring at the same time. Hillary was his dearest, perhaps his only friend—but Lord, how exasperating she could be sometimes!

"I didn't feel up for the fête, and Da had given me the day to myself, 'cause he didn't want me hangin' 'bout his stall and ruining business. So I lit out for the Barrens to see what my soul looks like."

"There you go, feeling sorry for yourself again, Ian."

"Well, bloody lot to feel sorry for, ain't there, Hiller?" He turned and stared vacantly at the clutter of odds and ends collected about this makeshift room: an old broken chair; a torn tapestry depicting jousting knights; rumpled rugs. "Besides," he continued lowly, "I hate to watch people have fun."

"What a mordant bastard! So what happened on the Barrens?" She was busy pouring water into tin cups from a skin bag.

"To begin with, poor Night tagged along and got himself dead."

Hillary spilled a splash of water. "Night! What happened? Oh God—the knacker will boil your bones. And the poor dear dog!"

Ian sat up and grabbed his cup of water. His throat was dry, and he slaked his thirst before telling the tale. Then he told it.

"A princess, you think? Named Alandra," Hillary interrupted. "And a wound? Let me see?"

" 'Tis nothing. I can't even feel it. Scabbed. Will do for now."

"And the thing that gave you this wound . . . the one sunk in the mire. You called it a Narx?"

"Norx. From the Black Circle. If not for me, the woman's horse wouldn't have fallen off that cliff. She'd be here now, under Baron Richard's protection." He slapped himself sharply on the head. "Dumb oaf!"

"This woman—a princess, you say," said Hillary softly. "Was she very beautiful, Ian?"

Ian sighed wistfully. "Yes. She was that, Hiller. Blue eyes, deeper than the sky just after sunset."

"Bluer than my eyes, Ian?" said Hillary in a tiny voice.

"Oh, indeed. And a noble face and fine figure and long blond hair that reaches out and grabs you by the heart." Ian closed his eyes and slouched back, recollecting the beauty and his attendant emotions. "Aye, I've never seen one so lovely, Hiller. Not in all my born days, I haven't!"

Hillary was quite silent, but Ian did not notice. His aches and pains were ebbing; regret was flowing strongly once more. The strange woman was gone forever like a fulfilling dream swallowed up by black nightmare. It was simply too much to bear. He needed some sort of relief to assuage this guilt.

He went to a chest and drew out a small cask of brown ale. Prizing the cork out, he took a long cool drink, feeling the coolness change to welcome expansive warmth in his stomach. "Want some, Hiller?"

The girl had her head turned away. She leaned against her knees. Her voice had a quavering quality. "No. Not now."

Ian downed another gulp of the yeasty stuff, belched, and continued his tale.

"Ian," Hillary interrupted at the bit about his decision to seek help from knights. "In God's sweet name, why didn't you come to me first? You know they can't understand you!" There were traceries of glistening moisture about her eyes, drying tracks down her reddened cheeks, one on either side of her stumpy nose.

"Can't you understand? I didn't think I had time enough to go looking for you, Hiller. I thought if I could stay calm and pronounce each of the words as clearly as I could, they would understand me."

"You are so dense, Ian!" Hillary said, shaking her head and placing it back upon her knees. "They don't want to understand you. Get that into your thick skull, instead of beating your head against the brick wall of their hatred!"

Ian gripped the cask wretchedly. "But they will understand me, one of these days. They will care about me. Can't they see I'm really no different from them? You can see, Hiller. Why can't they? Why do they taunt and jeer at me, just because I look and sound funny? Why, Hiller? Why?" He took a consoling slurp of brew. It bubbled up his throat and through his nostrils. He wiped his nose on his shirt, coughing. "Well, I don't care. I just don't care anymore, so let 'em bloody hang twisting in the wind, if it were up to me!"

The girl was quiet a moment, gnawing pensively at the woolen fabric of her blue shirt sleeve. "So," she said finally. "You went to the knights in front of the Crowing Cock and tried to tell them your fantastic story about a bunch of horsed monsters carrying off a beautiful distressed damsel into the Dark Circle. Even if they understood, do you think they'd have believed you?"

"Don't you believe me, Hiller?" Ian looked up, a pang in his throat.

"Of course I believe you, silly. You've a wonderful imagination, but even you couldn't make up a story like this. I'm just saying that those puffed-up kingsmen wouldn't have believed you anyway, even if they could make out what you said. And by the way, how the devil did you take care of that dandy who was drubbing you so spectacularly?"

"I don't know, Hiller." Ian shrugged, scratching his hip, which itched. "I suppose I figured that if I could take care of that Norx, I could as least face Godfrey. I was just lying there, eating dirt—and before I knew what was happening, I did it!"

"I've never seen you so agile, so quick, Ian. You were like lightning. You were absolutely wonderful!"

"Was I?" said Ian, pleased. "Yes, I suppose I

was, wasn't I?" His hand hit his dangling pouch, felt the thin rod it held. "Hillary. I forgot. Take a look at this strange thing I found in the square. I think that little man playing Laslo the Wandering Angel dropped it." He picked the metal cylinder from his pocket, examined it, then handed it to Hillary.

She held it by the candle flame. "My goodness. I've never seen the like before!" The shiny gold of it gleamed in the smoky light.

"That little stud atop it—press!"

Hillary put a thumb on top and pressed. With a click the nozzlelike projection suddenly appeared. Hillary felt it with her forefinger, then dropped the rod to the floor, staring in horror at her finger. "Ian! It spat a blue line on me! Look!" She showed Ian the pad of her finger, and sure enough, there was a thin solid blue line drawn across the breadth.

"Does it hurt, Hiller?"

"Why—no. No, not at all."

"What do you think, Hill?" Ian said in somber tones, picking the cylinder back up from the floor. "You think it's . . . magic?"

"Ninny. You know magic doesn't work except within the Dark Circle."

"Yes, but legend says that sometimes very strong magic will work occasionally, if it's close enough to the border. Do you think this is a magic wand? You think maybe it helped me beat Godfrey Pinkham?"

"You knew that knight?"

"Back when I was younger, he used to come

to our neighborhood and play God with us kids. We really thought he was something special, with his fine silk clothes and his haughty manner. He picked on me all the time, and everyone enjoyed that immensely."

"Poor Ian," said Hillary, patting his hand. "Well, you showed him today, you did, though you're going to have to keep out of sight of those kingsmen for a fortnight or so. As to this cylinder . . . I really can't say, but it hasn't done harm yet, so I'd keep it."

"Maybe, if it were a magic wand, I could set off after Alandra myself and rescue her!"

Hillary's light blue eyes lit with amusement. "Dear Ian. You are a romantic deep down, aren't you?"

"Of course not!" cried Ian indignantly. "I'm just trying to make amends for the stupid thing I did. For my cowardice. I'm no romantic. And dammit, no matter what this flimsy body does, I'm no coward either! I swear I'm not, and I'm going to prove it! To everyone. Don't you see—I have to, or I'll hate myself forever! I've got to beat this timid side to me."

"I know you're no coward, Ian!" said Hillary. "You don't need to show me . . . nor that Norx nor Godfrey what's-his-name or his clinking, drunken friends after today. As for the woman, it wasn't your fault!"

"If only I had given challenge to those creatures as she asked me to! If only I had stood my ground!" He sipped his ale again. "She would have gotten away!"

"And you'd be out there now, rotting in the Barrens, slashed to pieces. From what you say, they'd have cut you to bows and ribbons in a second and then galloped on to capture the woman anyway. Your fit was a blessing this time, Ian. Not a curse. You're alive, dear. And that's all that counts."

"No, it's not!" cried Ian, feeling the effects of the ale. "No, it's not, if you've got to live feeling the way I do now."

"I understand."

"No, you don't. No one understands. No one knows what it's like to be a misshapen, ugly monster ... with a weak will on top of it. A dog had to save my life, Hillary."

"We'd better just not mention we even saw Night today, Ian, or the knacker will assume it's your fault the dog is gone."

"Well, it is my fault."

"Just the same," Hillary replied soothingly. "Best not to even mention it. Neither repentance nor confession is going to stitch Night back into one piece again. And please, Ian," she continued, running a small hand down his side comfortingly. "Don't blame yourself. If you had your way, you'd have everyone believe that it's your fault the way you are! That you're being punished for some obscure sins! Well, it's just not true. You're a good person. I don't care if no one else knows that, only me. It doesn't make it any the less true that I'm the only one perceptive enough to realize your worth."

Ian had heard the speech before. He refused to let it improve his mood, preferring long gulps of his ale. Action bore out truth, not simple being. He had to show everyone his worth, not simply keep it to himself. And, by God, he would. He promised himself that he would indeed. Most of all, he would show Hillary that he was capable of breaking through to the rest of them. Sometimes he had the claustrophobic feeling that the young girl reveled in the fact that she alone could fully communicate with him. It was as though he were some sort of pet, to be whispered to and cuddled and molly-coddled despite its ugliness . . . perhaps because its ugliness made it hers alone.

Hillary Muffin was a blacksmith's daughter from down Potter's Lane. Ian had known her since she was a toddler and he was nine, which perhaps was why the bond of her friendship with him was so strong. She hadn't had a chance to observe his freakish differences before she had grown to care for him. It was quite curious with little Hillary Muffin: She had taken to him immediately, as animals tended to, her childish, wide eyes astounded by the first sight of him, her pudgy little hand reaching to take his hand, demanding communication and attention and simultaneously extending an invitation to share her limited experience and her delighted awe with life. Since then, theirs had been a happy and close relationship; now, somehow, Ian found it confining despite the comfort it offered.

Hillary treated him as an equal. He resented the fact that no one else did, and sometimes his resentment spilled on the poor girl's head.

Besides, what did she know? She was only fifteen.

Through his growing alcoholic haze, he examined the girl. Her wiry red hair was mussed, like a lopsided ball embedded on her round skull above the low brow and babyish features. She was friend, confidante, sister, and companion. Yet somehow he wanted more; and from someone else.

"I think I'll take a snooze," he said.

"You do that," she said, looking about for a blanket to cover him. "I'll wake you before sunset, so you can get home to dinner."

He was already asleep; her words were lost on him.

She found the threadbare blanket and swept it over him, covering his battered clothing attentively.

"Somebody has to take care of you, Ian," she whispered quietly, stroking his stiff, ratty hair. "Somebody has to."

Smiling to herself, she lay down beside his snoring, stinking, crooked body and continued her vigil.

The rook was black as the darkest dark between the stars. Like a piece of premature night seeking shelter from the afternoon sun, it fluttered through the wood's shadows. It hovered a moment, then settled on a low elm branch to scout for food.

Hunger gnawed within its small stomach; it had not eaten since early morning, and the worms it had tugged from damp ground had been underfleshed. It cocked a watchful eye along the weedy overgrowth of the forest floor for some hapless beetle or juicy cockroach.

Scent rather than sight attracted its attention. The smell of blood. Fresh blood, painting the breeze invitingly. The rook was not revulsed by carrion; it took its meals where it could, and if the flesh it smelled was some time dead, well . . . a little aging never hurt. Ruffling well-preened feathers, canting its head this way and that to zero in upon the potential food's location, the bird took a moment to consider.

There it was—by that oddly bent oak. A splotch of scarlet. Could it be anything but blood? And blood certainly indicated bone and sinew. With a squawk, the rook flapped down, perching on a length of twisted root. It looked this way and that, as precaution against prowling predators of the ground. Finding nothing threatening, it gave the ground a good examination with one eye.

It did not have to search long. Dinner was as healthy a portion of sinew and skin as the bird had ever seen. The rook cawed with excitement, hopped down, and proceeded to peck. This close, the flesh was a touch green, true. As was the blood. But no matter . . . it tasted all right.

The rook beaked down a munchy length of

vein, considering the strange form of this bit of meat. A thick torso, with five appendages of various lengths. The bird gave the rookish equivalent of a shrug and proceeded with its repast.

The hand twitched.

Once, twice it shuddered, and before the rook could jump back or take off, the thing righted itself and grabbed the black bird.

The rook was aware of a powerful squeeze. A red film flowed across its eyes.

Then nothing.

A mouth opened in the palm of the hand. It proceeded to devour the bird.

When it was finished, having downed flesh, feathers, eyes, bones, and beak alike, it crawled away, using five digits, in search of more food.

chapter eight

It was tough being a medieval guy, especially a malformed medieval guy with a speech impediment in a land that placed high value on grandioquence.

Sited on the edge of magic as it was, closer than most fiefdoms, Mullshire was fairly rife with legend. Speaking little, Ian had learned the advantage of listening, so he was a walking encyclopedia of the tales he had heard, the whispered myths, the street rumors. Many of these concerned different kinds of communities, communities with forms of government different from feudalism.

He liked these stories and would dream of distant places where there were no knights, no serfs, no barons, no kings; for some reason, he just did not feel comfortable in the kind of society he lived in.

Feudalism, of course, was tantamount to religion in the Outlying Kingdoms Without Magic. The reason was simple enough: It worked. People seemed pleased with their mostly mean, sometimes roisterous, quite short lives. Ian had heard legends of other lands where there was no hunger or filth, where there was pleasurable work and love enough to spare, and where, from time to time, the denizens would hold medieval festivals, play medieval roles and games, forge tales of medieval valor and glory. What stupid people, Ian Farthing thought. This is a rotten life.

So, when he had the opportunity to do something to change that life, he decided to take it. Only he wasn't going to be stupid this time, burbling garbled entreaties in front of boorish knights at the Crowing Cock. No, he was going to a Great Authority. He and Hillary had worked out a plan before he had gone back to his home. Today was the first of the joust days, where demented knights would clobber hell out of each other with all manner of ponderous weaponry—and Baron Richard was quite fond of the spectacle.

However, the first obstacle to this plan was Ian's stepfather, Soames Farthing. Ian was ready to seize opportunity by the scruff of the neck when the old man stumbled into his room just before dawn to wake him.

"Get your lazy bum out o' the sack, churlish lout," the whiskered man growled, weaving over his adopted son's bed. "Ye've got a full day's worth of shoes to mend." The odor of drink was ripe on the man's breath; clearly he was just coming in from a long night at one of the lowlier inns. "Your dear mum's got some mash for breakfast."

When Ian sat down for his meal, his father was snoring into his arms at the table. His mother stood at the stove, stirring a pot of gruel.

"Ye'll eat your fill of this nourishing stuff, then, Ian!" she said. "You ate poorly last night, even though your absent father's portion was at hand."

"Absent still, isn't he?" Ian said, clumping down at the table. The tremor this produced in the wood caused Farthing senior to rouse for a bare moment, then sink back into a gentle snoring.

"There, there," the old woman said, ladling a ghastly mess of boiled roughage into Ian's bowl. "Fill your mouth with porridge, not foul talk of your father. He's a hard life and he deserves a night in his cups from time to time."

Ian's nervous stomach was barely able to handle a mouthful of the gunk; but he ate it to satisfy his mum, whose help he needed. "Mum," he said. "You must help me speak with Da. He understands me poorly, and I have an idea for him."

"If ye can wake him," his mother said, wiping rough hands on her apron. "Ye'll have my mouth, Ian, on the condition that you'll eat every speck of that breakfast." Hands on hips emphasized the severity of the woman's determination that the gruel be transferred from bowl through jowl to bowel.

Ian choked some more food down, drank some water, then poured the rest of the cold cup's contents on his father's head. "Heaven take me, I am so sorry, Father!"

Farthing senior grumbled up blearily, water runneling down wrinkled face. "Your fits will be my doom, Ian," he murmured. Before he could sink back to slumber, however, his wife grabbed him by the collar and bellowed in his ear.

"Soames, Ian wishes to speak to you."

"Da, a fabulous idea has come to me, and we shall make much money by it. I shall this day, with your permission, take a cart filled with tools and supplies to the gaming grounds. Jousts are terribly hard on people's feet; and there are sometimes long waits between bouts. In this manner, I shall offer quick footwear mending at a reasonable price to the dozens in need, and turn a pretty profit."

"Ye've shoes to mend at home," the cobbler growled after listening to his wife's translation.

"Aye, but there'll be no one coming to pick them up for days. Plenty of time during Festival, when no one thinks to prance themselves to a cobbler's shop."

"No good will come of the likes of you gimping about with our valuable barrow at the games!" the worthy pronounced.

"I have procured, Da, the services of my friend Hillary to help for less than a pittance. After your nap, you yourself may come and check on my progress. Perhaps we shall even earn enough to buy you an ale barrel at Festival prices."

Mr. Farthing belched, then eyed his apprentice suspiciously. "It's a dog's moon when you're so industrious, my son. What's the occasion?"

"Ah, and there's part of the deal, Da. I turn sufficient coin this day, and I get a pittance above my regular allowance."

"And why not?" Mum tacked on, after translating. "I think it's a splendid idea, Harry, as long as Ian carries along a nice parcel of my cold porridge to nourish him!"

The cobbler rubbed his greasy whiskers, then grinned maliciously. "Aye, a skinny thing is Ian, and hard to make to eat thy excellent vittles, madam. So in the interest of all, I'll strike a deal then, my scruffy son! Take another helping of breakfast now, and take with thee plenty of porridge with the promise on they mother's distant grave that ye'll eat it all up afore sundown, and I'll permit ye to carry out this mercenary endeavor."

Ian Farthing's stomach grumbled in abject protest, but he could do nothing but agree.

This wisdom of Solomon properly dispensed, Soames Farthing avoided his own bowl of porridge by going back to sleep.

A bright dawn found Ian Farthing, cart in tow, knocking at Hillary Muffin's door.

A head poked out of a window. "Shhhhh!" Hillary cried. "Mother and Father are still asleep."

"Then ye can go?"

"They didn't say I couldn't!" Hillary said brightly. "Hold a moment. I'll change."

Ian slouched at the doorstep, rubbing his punished abdomen, wondering if he would compromise his word to his parents by sticking a finger down his throat and ridding himself of the wretched gunk in his belly that seemed to have congealed into stone. His contemplations, however, were interrupted by a harsh voice calling his name.

"Here! Farthing! Look alive, cobbler's son, and be attentive!"

Ian turned to find himself being addressed by Hank Markson the knacker, pulling a cart. Heaped upon the cart were the bodies of dead animals.

"Good business this morn, and most free," Hank commented, seeing the direction of Ian Farthing's attention. He slapped away flies with a piece of tanned hide. "Amazing how many pets get trampled or run over come Festival time. Or find themselves victim to drunken pranks. Prowl the morning alleys, and shovel 'em up. Got a few rats in here, I do, but cats and dogs mostly, poor fellas." Hank the knacker prided himself that all his clothing was of noble material, albeit at least fourth-hand and threadbare. For all the patches, though, the way he carried himself he could have been a prince. The common jokes about Hank were about the airs he took on, odoriferous and otherwise.

Ian looked away from the cartful of dead and stiffening animals, grabbing his nose and deciding gagging was less pleasant than hanging on to breakfast. "Hallo, Hank."

"And speaking of dogs in particular," the middle-aged man said, scratching his paunch, "I don't suppose you've seen that mutt of mine, Night. I know he hangs about you sometimes. Ain't seen him since yesterday morn. Happy to say he ain't in the mornin' gatherings."

Ian shook his head.

"I told him, 'Now, you shouldn't be dogging that strange lad's heels or you'll run afoul.' And there is the witch's touch on you, lad, and I don't know if it's good or bad, but that's why I keep me distance." He touched a red round nose. "The nostrils can smell out the fairy dust, even through all my precious simmerings. And so Night's a good dog, and should I find he's spell-taken, I'll be speakin' with your da, Ian Farthing. Or maybe I'll get meself a nice new lump of ugly gristle for me pots, eh!"

Ian turned away, trying not to shudder with the thought.

At his moment, Hillary Muffin bounced out the door, smiling, face freshly scrubbed. "And a good morning to ye, mistress," the knacker said, taking off his cap in mock deference. "I don't suppose you've anything dead you'd care to dispose of?"

Hillary blanched at the sight of the dead animals. "Not at the moment, Hank."

"Remember, Farthing. You catch sight of me dog, you send him runnin' back to me yard forthwith!" So saying, the knacker proceeded to rattle down Elbow Lane, careful not to lose one precious rat from his collection.

"Goodness, Ian," Hillary said, blue eyes wide. "You don't suppose . . ."

"Idle threats," Ian said, trying to convince himself. "How could that fellow possibly know what happened to Night? No way he'll find out, either." He hoisted himself creakily to his feet. "To the gaming fields, then, Hiller!" he said, trying to sound cheerful. "Give us a hand . . . this cart is heavy!"

"I rather hoped for a ride, Ian!" she said playfully, skipping around the cart, long skirts flouncing fetchingly.

"It's going to be a long day and I've no intention of expending my energies carrying a willful strumpet in me cart!"

"Ian Farthing, such a way with words." She took one handle of the cart. "Let us merely hope that Baron Richard listens to a few."

"Aye, Hiller, but we can only do our best and pray that's what will be the return." He patted a pocket of his jerkin. "I've that possibly magic wand here for the chance of good luck."

"Your luck and my pluck, Ian Farthing," she said as the lad picked up his handle. "What a fine team we make!"

Ian shook his head woefully as they made their way toward the fields.

Chapter nine

Lady Alandra, Queen of the Dawn, Thrice-Blessed Jewel Princess of the Rainbow, Key to Unknown Doorways, and Wife to Morgsteen, the most powerful Lord of the Dark Circle, awoke that morning feeling awful.

Morning light slipped through the mist rings around the mountains in slanted rays, emphasizing the monochromatic character of this grim land. The only bit of color that livened anything up was her bright clothing, and that was getting wretchedly ratty.

What was a girl to do without the right set of clothes? She really should have packed something else besides this beastly gown. But then how could she have possibly known that the opportunity for escape would be handed to her on a silver platter at such an inopportune moment as the Grand Escapade of Shirth, the Ball of the Astrologers? Of course, all that Zodiac business was stuff and nonsense, but then it was a perennial prerequisite for the diviners at court, a chance to dance and frolic amid spe-

cial alignments of the confused constellations
above the Dark Kingdom. If only her runes had
spoken up a little sooner, she might at least
have worn breeches and blouse beneath this
accursed gown!

Her runes!

The thought caused her hand to reach for the
pouch that should be dangling from her belt.
And yes, they were still there, stones snug in
their sack.

She looked over to the Norx. Tombheart still
slept, while Toothmaw stood watch, occasionally flicking his dead eyes her way to make
sure she hadn't taken a hike.

Yes, she would have a moment to consult
her runes. She prayed to the Higher Gods she
didn't really believe in that the Norx wouldn't
take her stones away from her. Their thorough-
ness no doubt had recognized their harmless-
ness; such small stones could do no harm without a sling. And perhaps they knew of her
personal attachment to the runes. They were a
part of her Key-ness. . . . Although Heaven knew
what that meant. Morgsteen went on and on
about that subject. As far as Alandra knew,
thought, or cared, she was just a normal princess doomed to a rotten marriage, victim of
some kind of infernal prophecy. She just wanted
to get away from it all and enjoy life. What was
wrong with enjoying life?

She turned away from the Norx's view so that
she could commune with her runes untroubled.
She untied the black velvet pouch, undid the
drawstrings, then shook them awake.

Tiny squabbling sounds came from the sack. Confounded sleepy things!

She opened the top and spoke into the darkness. "Front and center, you jerks. You got me into a big mess and I want to get out!"

Whisperings and clickings ensued. She gave them a moment to align, then stuck three fingers into the pouch. "Upsy-daisy!" she ordered.

A stone slipped into her grasp. She brought it into the light. The stone was a flat sandstone, with a symbol cut into one face. Alandra recognized it immediately . . . it was Roach, rune of Goof-ups, Improprieties, and Mistakes.

"So what went wrong, huh?" she demanded in a harsh whisper, then put the stone up against her ear.

"Your highness," a squeaky voice began nervously, "we runes request your forgiveness. We poor penitent lumps of worthless rock beg that you not cast us into the depths to while away eternity in watery darkness. Oh pretty princess . . . I mean, great queen, we renew our vows of eternal servitude, only voice your redemptive healing pardon upon these worthless lumps—"

"Shut up and tell me what went wrong!"

"Ah! You are not going to cast us away from your delightful bosom?"

"Of course not, you ninny. Not when it took me half my childhood finding you on my Treasure Hunt. Some treasure, though!"

"Oh, excellent. The others will be so relieved. Please place me back and draw another one of us!"

She followed directions, and found herself holding the symbol of a mouth, reversed. Orata, the rune of Explanations, Speech, and Language.

"Fourscore and seven years ago," it said, then cleared its metaphorical throat. "Yes, quite. I have nothing to offer but blood, sweat, and—"

"How about something a little more concrete, like the reason you turkeys made such a big deal about me skedaddling when this was going to happen?"

"Sticks and stones, madam!" pronounced the rune stentoriously. "As it happens, my fellows and I were just involved in a conference on that very matter, and we should like the opportunity of a little more time to consider the subject, with the aid of a mere moment of cooperation on your part!"

"Like what?"

"Come, come, my dear! You need not address me in such a cynical tone. Take heart! Remember, dust to dust and ashes to ashes, scrapes and pricks are better than rashes!"

"I haven't got time for gobbledygook, Orata. I'll do what you want me to do."

"Very well, madam. We should like you to concentrate on yester eve's festivities, when you made the unfortunate decision to bolt from your husband's manse!"

"Me? Decide? You told me to, you ninny! You and your mineral monkeybrains said that it was the best time!"

"Ah, but remember, oh great queenie, we only give advice. You need not take it."

Alandra sighed. "Very well. I'm upset, though, and it's hard to concentrate."

"We shall exert our poor energies, madam, to the very utmost that you may perceive truly and correctly, if you would simply place the pouch near your forehead."

Alandra placed the bag of stones near her forehead, closed her eyes, and remembered how it had been:

"Oh, my lovely piece of Heaven, molded into female form," said Snirk Morgsteen, reaching out with his long, snaky fingers. "May I help you slip that delightful body into that lovely dress?"

Somehow, whenever he got lovelorn, Morgsteen's usual leer on his ratlike face grew larger, smarmier. Alandra, towel wrapped around her shapely form, suppressed a shudder as she saw who awaited her in her dressing room. "My lord," she said through gritted teeth. "Is it the custom of Blankshun that a husband should intrude upon his lady's toilet? As you can see, and as my lady-in-waiting can attest, I have just taken my bath in preparation for the astrological festivities you have planned for this evening."

"Ah, my cherry creampuff, if I were permitted into your toilet, I would hand you your toilet paper!" The skinny man, finery folded about him like oily rodent skin, grasped his wife's hand and began to kiss it ardently, managing to smear it with spittle in the process.

"Ah, sweet dumpling breasts, your exquisite smells inspire me to ecstasy! Tell me that tonight, after three months of waiting, we can finally share in the consumption of our marriage!"

"Consummation, my lord, I believe is the correct term," said Queen Alandra. "Dear heart, you know that just as soon as my internal peregrinations are aright, I shall gladly submit to the full attentions of your manly . . . dispositions." She turned and winked at Shirliq, her lady-in-waiting. "But how many times must I explain that the first time must be chosen with discretion, lest the forces that swirl within me gallop unchecked and, in mid-congress, wrest thy manly attributes from between thy very legs! Or imbue them with some horrid pox! Or rot them with some forgotten spell! Remember, King Morgsteen, that I am the Key, and my maidenhead is not to be taken lightly."

Morgsteen cringed a moment at the thought of the possible dire consequences. "My queen, you cannot understand the tides of desire that churn in my bowels!"

"Patience, patience, Snirky, my fond, dear love," Alandra said, inwardly breathing a sigh of relief. She was back in control again. "Once we have gotten past our little magical dilemma, I shall no doubt be under the spell of passion, and demand use of your obvious virility constantly!" She let the towel drop a bit to underscore her promise. "Oh, dear, but you must not see me this way!"

Morgsteen's Adam's apple bobbed as he swallowed hard at the sight of his pure maiden's feminine attributes. "Forgive me, but I have forgotten myself! I did not come to your chamber in the ardent state I find myself in now. My alchemists request that you wear your golden gown this evening, my dear. I thought I might bring you that message personally."

"Oh, bother," Alandra said, walking behind her dressing screen. "I had my heart set on the chartreuse affair with the frills!"

"You forget, my pumpkin," Morgsteen said, "that this is no normal festivity, but a celebration of the Magical Eyes that see into our Destiny. And so you and I must bow to the requests of those seers and sorcerers who have made possible my power, and will help deliver to me what I wish."

"Isn't the lion's share of the Dark Circle sufficient, my kingly Snirky?"

"You know it is not, else I would not have taken such pains, made such sacrifices of lives and material, to win you, Alandra," Morgsteen said soberly. "You, after all, are the Key."

"Alandra the Key," said the lady-in-waiting. "Perhaps the seers mispronounced at their divinations and truly meant Alandra the Coy!"

"Are your torturers busy by any chance, Snirky?" Alandra growled, shooting Shirliq a nasty look.

Morgsteen seemed lost in thought. "What magical role you play no one knows yet, but the portents show that he who owns you,

Alandra, will own the path to True Power, True Destiny! And I have sworn on my father's immortal soul to avenge his death and live to achieve what he sought. Total and absolute control of this bedeviling magic that flits through our lives like gnats at times, like bats, or like doves at daybreak. That tortures us with pain and beauty. I have sworn to tame this land, Alandra, and with you, and my troops of sorcerers, I shall fight fire with greater fire!"

"Very well. The gold it will be." She flung the towel over the screen. It caught her husband in the face. "Now please depart, husband. A woman must have her privacy, after all, if she is to represent her king properly at a ball!"

Morgsteen bowed obsequiously and departed.

"Bleeccchhhh!" said Alandra. "Shirliq, touching that man is like getting intimate with a collection of bound-together eels!"

"Your aversion is apparent, my lady," said the lady-in-waiting. "But how much longer can you avert his advances? You know as well as I do that the maidenhead you refer to has long ago entered the province of myth."

"Hmm, yes, and most delightfully as well. Such a shame that dear Roger died defending me."

"He would have died anyway, I fear, had he known of the divers lovers you have taken in his absence. It is fortunate indeed that your father had the forethought to bribe the Registrar of Mystical Peccadilloes before Morgsteen stormed your keep and claimed you as his own."

"My departed father did no such thing!" Alandra said mischievously. "It was a simple matter of rewriting my records myself, with a little help from the rather lecherous registrar. Indeed, this is the reason why Morgsteen is convinced of the truth concerning my virginity and its explosive nature. I myself penned that document!" She stormed out from behind the screen, wearing a pale gray shift, stomping about in frustration in the royal dressing room decked with lace and color. She gazed out the window onto the misty sweep of the moors and mountains of the Dark Land. "Oh, but I cannot wait much longer. I must know . . ."

"Perhaps your runes will either direct your steps or calm you, milady."

"My runes! Of course!" She went to her dresser and pulled out her bag, shook it up, "Front and center!" she cried, pulling out one of her stones.

It was Stup, the rune of Misdirection, Confusion, and Realignment.

"Dear Alandra," it said, "the others wish me to inform you that you are having the wrong memory flashback."

"Oh," she said.

"Please go forward a few hours to the ball, when we performed our little . . . ah . . . indiscretion."

The dressing room dissolved, to be replaced by the sweep and sound of a dance in the Royal Palace. Magical pipes skirled through the hall, echoing with thrilling pirouettes of mel-

ody and harmony, blending in a cadenced
rhythm, the beats to which costumed attendees
swayed in stately frolic.

Alandra found herself once more in her golden
gown, clean and sparkling now, conversing with
a handsome numerologist on the thaumaturgical
implications of a null set, when suddenly her
rune pouch began to slap against her side
insistently.

"Will you excuse me?" she said charmingly.
"I must see to a privy duty!"

"I believe, your highness," said the man, a
sparkle in his eyes, "that you have my number."

Alandra rushed away toward a place where
she could answer a different call, but Morgsteen
intercepted her.

"My dear, I have heard nothing but ravishing
things about your conduct tonight. You are an
ornament in my crown to be prized above all.
Now, you simply must meet a new appretice
sorcerer I have enlisted, who is working on the
very puzzle that concerns you the most."

"Oh, gladly, my lord," she said, fidgeting.
"But I have drunk too much wine and the toll
keeper demands his price for my overindul-
gence."

"The Royal Compartment is at your disposal,"
said Morgsteen.

Alandra flinched. "Oh my, but you know
how I hate those Norx who guard it. No, really,
the normal privy will do quite well, Snirky."

"Oh, but I insist!" he said, taking her firmly
by the hand and guiding her up past the nor-

mal guards and down a hall toward his Royal Personal Latrine, where stood the fulsome Norx guards, Murklung and Tombheart. "And just to think!" he said jokingly, pointing at the entrance. "As some dead poet once said, 'Mark but this privy, and mark in this, how little that which thou deniest me is!' "

"Please," said Alandra. "Fleas are bad enough!"

She went into the royally appointed privy after parting with a quick kiss to assuage her husband, and found a private compartment.

"Okay, okay, so stop the ruckus! You're gonna make my thigh black and blue!" she said, unfastening the bag and opening it up. She picked out a stone, which proved to be Iris, the rune of Reception, Perception, and Appreciation.

"This is it!" Iris whispered in her ear. "I'm getting it all again. Yes, yes, everything is right. Our instructions that you immediately climb into the royal stables and mount your horse and dash for the Portal are perfectly correct!"

"So then what went wrong?" she demanded impatiently.

"Shift forward a few moments and we'll see what you've got in your memory," the rune instructed.

Alandra concentrated her thoughts upon the near future and instantly the contorted royal plumbing fixtures surrounding her flushed away, spilling her atop the saddle of Crackers, whom she had filched from the stables. She galloped through the darksome street, avoiding the shifting forms of the wraiths that prowled the alleys, green eyes watching hungrily. Onward to the sacred ground, the Cairn Mounds, where a squad of Norx guarded the Portal.

Crackers's charge took the monsters by surprise; with a swirl of cape and jab of spurs the magnificent black beast hurtled the fence and was halfway up the hill before the creatures could react.

The runes jangled insistently.

It was difficult to draw a rune from a pouch atop an equine express, especially if you're only a memory, but somehow she managed it just as Crackers almost obtained the blurry mist center of the diamond Portal.

"This is the moment," the jabbering voices of the runes seemed to whisper. "We feel the energies!"

She pulled the stone from the pouch, and, she remembered, time suddenly froze all about her. A powerful charge raced up her hand as she held the stone, like a stream of electricity—but despite the pain, she held onto the stone, as the doughnut shape of the Portal dissolved into the milk of memory.

As though awakened from a dream, Alandra found herself back upon her blanket, holding a stone. . . .

No, two stones!

Two of the runes had somehow fused together! Grimm, Declarer of Catastrophe and Disruption, and the most powerful rune of all, Cypher, the rune of Nothingness.

"Oh, mortification," growled the bass whisper of Grimm. "Cheek to jowl with Sir Zilch!"

"You think I'm enjoying this?" Cypher responded. "My happiest moments are when your ponderous portents are well to the other side of the bag!"

"Shut up and let me know what has happened and what I must do!" Alandra insisted.

"Well, milady," ground the stone named Grimm, "things are in bad shape, and that's no fairy tale!"

"Don't you think I know that, lunkhead? What did you see?" Alandra demanded harshly.

It was Cypher's turn to speak. "Knowing nothing, I am closer to the truth than most of my companions, and, in truth, the general consensus is that someone threw a monkey wrench into the gears of Cosmic Entropy."

"To extend the miserable metaphor, madam," Grimm continued, "a couple of cogs consequently cracked!"

"What the alliterate means," said Cypher, "is that our analysis of the distortion indicates it was nothing random, but the beginning of a greater pattern."

"Okay, so some wizard somewhere is gunking things up. What does that mean to me? What should I do?"

"That, we fear, at the moment is unclear," replied Cypher. "But because of your Keyness in the scheme of things, we presume you are of at least peripherally Central Importance."

"Nothing else?" Alandra said. "What good are you?"

"A few images, madam, is all," Grimm said. "Images of a certain fellow of tantamount importance to your future."

"A hero? My savior?" Alandra asked eagerly.

"Well, not precisely. He seems a very twisted sort. Physical problems, don't you know, but the emanations from this image are strong, quite strong, and if you do another quick casting, I do believe you might get some sort of an idea as to the nature of the man."

Alandra placed the recently joined stones back into their place and took out another stone. She sighed.

"Great Queen," a voice rumbled behind her. She turned to find Tombheart standing over her. "If you will prepare to renew our journey, we shall spare a few of our delicious dried sweetworms to satisfy your morning appetite."

"How delightful," she said, and, under the supervision of the Norx, she prepared for the journey.

In the saddle, a thong tied around her middle and secured to Toothmaw's wrist, Alandra took out the rune she had drawn and placed it by her ear.

"Shoes," said the rune called the Fool. "I see lots and lots of shoes!"

chapter ten

"Look at all those feet, Hillary," Ian said as the crowds milled about the Gaming Field beside the mossy towers of Mullshire Castle. "Surely someone needs a shoe mended!"

Hillary jumped up and yelled, "Soles saved here! Save your soles here!" She smiled down at Ian from her perch atop the cart. "A little religion never hurt a sales campaign!"

Ian Farthing tapped his hammer impatiently. "Oh well, it was just a ruse to get us here. Too much work would have been a bad thing. Do you see the baron from up there?"

Hillary shielded her eyes from the sun and looked across the grassy sward toward where the gaily festooned royal reviewing stand had been set up. Armor glinted and clanked there, flags whipped in the breeze, but there was no sign of any royal personages to be had whatsoever.

"No, but I see weapons absolutely bristling, Ian! Maces and lances and morningstars and swords! And enough chainmail to choke a giant!"

"What kind of giant would want to eat chainmail, Hillary?"

"Just a figure of speech, Ian!"

"Well, as soon as you see any sign of the baron, we must take action before he's distracted by the jousts. The sooner he hears my pleas, the better!"

"Honestly, Ian, what do you expect him to do? Order up a squadron of his finest to go charging into the Dark Circle on the word of a questionable social figure?"

"Oh, Hiller! Can't you see? I must try." His voice was full of urgency. "I must attempt to right my follies!"

Hillary sighed. "Oh, very well, but all I can say is that I'm certainly glad you're clearly not the sort of physical specimen to be sent out on some harebrained quest for a stupid princess. This is where you belong, Ian, safe and productive, out of harm's way!"

"I told you, I held my own against that Norx!"

Hillary shivered. "It all sounds so perfectly dreadful. I need a sweet to calm my constitution." She took out a bit of candy and popped it into her mouth. Hillary was bonkers over sweets. Should Ian slave weeks over a leather bracelet or necklace as a gift, she would accept it thankfully and calmly; but gift her with a simple bag of sweets and she would be absolutely thrilled.

" 'ere you go, mate," a plump, brutish-looking farmer said, taking a sandal off and plopping it on the ground beside Ian's portable workbench. "Think you can mend that there thong?"

Ian grimaced at the reek that arose from the ancient leather. "Halfpence," he said, and Hillary translated.

"Right enough! That bugger's been slippin' and slidin' for nigh a week, and that's me good summer shoes! You fix them up aright, be mighty beholdin' to you!"

Ian selected a thick needle and study thread and commenced work, trying to ignore the odor. The farmer droned on, his breath yeasty with early brew intake from one of the many stalls. ". . . and I hear tell many a fine knight's goin' to take a plunge this day, and many a fine sight will be had, but I tell you, laddie and lady, these old eyes have seen a sight many a year ago like nothing anybody's ever seen afore, an' I don' mind telling it agin and agin and agin to my dying day." He scratched at whiskers, sounding like a wood file on sandpaper. "Ayup, I was tillin' me fields, you know, last bit of elbow grease at twilight just afore goin' home to the missus, when I hear a noise, and I look up. The sky had been clear before, but now there was this thundercloud a-brewin' just a rock's throw from me like some floatin' cow pie. And I says to meself, Jacob Tillster, this here is not a normal sight, this here. And then this cloud ignites with fire so bright, nearly blinded me poor plowman's eyes! An' with a crack like a toll ripped straight from Hell's bell, a rent opens up and these things fall out, including what looked like a kid, and . . ."

Ian, who had been paying scant attention, pulled the final stitch tight, then effected an expert knot. He handed the sandal back to the farmer, who stopped his tale when their eyes aligned. There was a momentary spark of something like recognition in the old farmer's eyes. Ian felt a peculiar feeling, which was interrupted by a tug on his jerkin.

"Ian! Ian, the baron's on his way. Let's pack up!"

"Ha'penny sir!" Ian managed to pronounce, holding out a flat palm. The man fumbled in his pocket and paid the cobbler. His gaze followed the young pair as they carried their cart toward where Baron Richard's retinue were ascending to their posts for convenient viewing of the festivities.

"Damme," the farmer said. "I seen them eyes afore. . . ."

Baron Richard Foxshot was a tall, graying man with eyes that darted about as though fearful of finding some plot afoot to overthrow him, or some assassin skulking about ready to put a quarrel between his shoulder blades. Notoriously absentminded, he was nonetheless a good ruler, fair, if highly traditional. Even though he often made known his dislike for the needlessly violent aspects of festivals, the common knowledge was that he actually relished every tournament. At the top of the stand, he took a moment to survey the knights in their preparation, the crowd in their anticipation, and was rewarded by the sight of a pair of scruffy craftspeople rolling a cart toward him, frantically waving and calling for his attention.

Immediately his bodyguards drew their swords, but he held up his hand, for he recognized the lad pulling the cart, and had a faint tremor of pity toward him. Some wrong toward the lad might be righted this day, and what better way to display it than this, before his multitude of vassals!

"Farthing I believe it is!" he said in his immaculate tenor. As hoped, the attention of his milling subjects was brought to the interchange. An excellent opportunity indeed! "The cobbler's son, who draws his fair share of trouble." To his guards: "No harm in the lad. I shall grant a short audience. Much more interesting, I think, than seeing my preening knights use one another for anvils!"

"Thank you, your highness," said Hillary, trembling a bit from a sudden nervousness. "Please excuse my humble self, but I have agreed to serve as Ian's mouth, since I am one of the few who can understand every word he says!"

"Ah, yes, that is correct, the horrid monster can't speak straight!"

"Horrid monster!" said Hillary indignantly. "He is nothing of the sort, you high-puffing—"

"Hillary," Ian said, "I don't care what he calls me. I just want to have my bloody say. Apologize!"

Hillary turned back to the baron. "I lost my

head, sir. Please, just lend us your ear, and you may then make your judgments and call your names."

"Fair enough," Baron Richard said, pulling out a silver snuffbox and sticking some up his nose. "Please pardon the anachronism, gentle people," he called out to the crowd, "but a splendid shipment of this stuff just came from the Black Circle, and I have grown quite fond of it! They say you can smoke it as well, but that's a little too much! Now then, where were we, young lady? Something important, I hope."

"Oh, very important, sir, so important that Ian attempted to seek the aid of some of your knights yonder and was most hideously treated."

Ian searched the grouping of knights, but he could not see Godfrey. He breathed a little easier.

The baron summoned one of his courtiers, and used the man's scarf to wipe his nose after a sneeze.

Hillary proceeded with the tale of the events that had occurred on the fringes of the Dark Circle, becoming sufficiently involved to act out sections of the drama. Her gestures and speech riveted those near enough to hear; her body English was enough to keep the attention of those farther away.

When her jumps and flourishes and her story were through, she received applause.

"And so you see, your majesty, Ian only wishes that his mistakes be corrected, and that this beautiful maiden be rescued. He hopes that perhaps a few knights might use the opportunity to form a quest for this royal personage!"

"A pretty tale," said Baron Richard. "But highly unlikely. Why should a lady of the Dark Circle of such importance seek shelter in our magicless town? I fear you have been taken in by Ian Farthing's imagination. And while it is appropriate for our entertainment of this day, I fear I can do nothing to help you." He raised his hands and clapped them together. "And now, if we can please get this over with, I have mounds of paperwork to attend to back in my study before tonight's drunken fest. You people may not realize it, but being a medieval despot takes a great deal of toil!"

Ian stumbled forward, aghast, tears in his eyes. "Oh, but Baron Richard, you must believe me, you must! All of my life has been a pathetic mess, and I must in some way redeem myself! Can't you see the courage it has taken on my part to address you so?"

But his words emerged garbled and tattered.

Baron Richard snapped his fingers. Crossbows leveled. "Step one step forward, beast, and you'll trouble no one anymore." He picked out a small gold coin from a pocket and tossed it to the gnarled fellow. "For the entertainment value alone, I assure you."

Ian did not pick up the coin, but turned away sadly and trudged off trailing his cart. Hillary, however, had the good sense to go and pick up the money. "Perhaps we can hire someone to help, and so we thank you for this, your grace."

Although his story was disbelieved roundly, the entertainment value attracted a number of customers to Ian's shoe repair cart. He hammered and mended glumly while the clanks and hoofbeats and the cheers from the tournament rose into the clear late-morning air.

There had been no wars to speak of in the past few years, and so the military folk drew special satisfaction from the increased frequency of such events, taking their blood and destruction and glory where they could. The armies of the manors and shires surrounding the Dark Circle served a twofold purpose. First and foremost, they guarded their shires from other armies. But also, from time to very occasional time, lords from the Dark Cricle emerged to hire them as mercenaries. In turn, when harvests were bad, or plague struck or any other manner of misfortune struck the surrounding nonmagical provinces, suddenly supplies would abruptly appear in communal larders, complete with detailed IOUs and reminders from their mysterious and sorcerous benefactors where their duties and loyalties lay.

The Mullshire Tournament Team was one of the very finest among the twenty provinces in the League of the Medieval Ring, and regularly achieved top ranking in the Knightly Olympics, hacking and slashing their way to statistical glory. Mullshire was a land of pure hometown spirit and regularly supported its lads in chain-mail with prayers and cheers.

So it was quite upsetting for all involved when, just in the middle of a particularly juicy joust, one of the Dark Lords came to call.

Baron Richard recognized the telltale death's head insignia on the ornithopter side as soon as the swishing of blades sounded over the field.

"Oh, damn!" he said, robes whipping in the wind. "Did I forget this month's taxes?"

"Sir," one of his courtiers said, "Kogar's protection monies were delivered in plenty of time. I have the receipt!"

The flying machine landed and a half-dozen Marines piled out holding machine guns.

"Ah, be a good fellow and go and get it, would you?" Baron Richard said.

Among the stalls, Ian Farthing looked up from his work. "What's all the commotion, Hillary?"

"Goodness, Ian! Some monster with swirling top wings landed in the gaming field."

"On top of Godfrey Pinkham, I hope!" Ian said, tossing the shoe back to the customer. "Let's have a gander, eh?"

They goosed a few bystanders to fight their way close to the source of excitement.

From the glass bubble compartment of the ornithopter, the Dark Lord known as Roth Kogar emerged, bumping his head in the process, but voicing no cry of pain. Kogar was a big, strapping fellow, his face a map of scars, his eyes like fires burning the parchment of that map.

His wild dark hair streamed about his head in bladebreeze as he casually drew his symbol of authority, his sword, and sauntered toward the reviewing stand.

"Right! Where is she?"

"Uhm, Lord Kogar, are you addressing me?" the baron asked meekly.

"No, I'm talking to myself, fool! Hand her over to me immediately, or I let some daylight into your guts!" He brandished the sword menacingly.

"My lord, who are you speaking of? Are you sure you have come to the right province? This is Mullshire, a demesne very faithful to the lords of the Dark Circle."

"I speak of Queen Alandra, of course!" Lord Kogar said. "According to my seers, she should at this very moment be secreted within your castle walls, and I've come for her, to do a favor for my dear friend Lord Morgsteen!"

"Alandra? I know of no Alandra." He gazed out hopefully upon his ranks of knights. "Anyone know of anyone named Alandra?"

Chainmail and helms clicked and clanked as heads shook.

"Well, there, you see!" the baron said, clearly feeling uncomfortably queasy at the abrupt visit of this Dark Lord with such a nasty reputation and disposition.

Lord Kogar swaggered back and forth, puffing and blowing. "By Beelzebub's corns, she's here somewhere! My seers and sages do not lie! I myself saw the message of destiny in the burst entrails of a spiff-lizard!" He swung to his men. "Give these sassy vassals a taste of hot lead straight from the Halls of Montezuma, men!"

The machine guns spat brief fire into a nearby crowd. People screamed, and fell doornail-dead.

"Ah, Lord Kogar," Baron Richard said, waving his hands frantically, "that really is not necessary! Please stop! I'm sure that if Queen Alandra is here, we can locate her! You're killing taxpayers!"

"By Heaven's outhouse, you're right," said Lord Kogar. "Nonetheless, I think that some kind of display of my power and might is necessary to teach you peons the occasional lesson. And my Marines do so love to serf!" An evil humor glinted in his eye. "I call upon the Ancient Rite of Trial by Battle to win the right to tear this town apart in search of Queen Alandra!"

"Lord Kogar, please!" Baron Richard said, face ashen and twitching. "This is really not necessary! I assure you that we will do everything in our power to complete the marvelous scouring you demand without—"

"By Satan's snot, silence, you knuffish haskard!" the Dark Lord bellowed in his rich baritone. "Indeed, I feel my oats this day, and would fain exercise myself. Besides, I always have deep respect for Ancient Rites. Why, just the other day a bunch of my druid friends and I got together and gave a hotfoot to a wonderful wicker man!" He waved his sword with the practiced ease of a master swordsman, or at the very least a fine chef. "So then, who will be the first young lad to challenge me?"

His vague memory took that moment to register on Ian Farthing. "Alandra! Hillary, that was the beautiful lady's name!"

"Ian, don't ..." Hillary cried, but she was too late to grab him before he hobbled out of the crowd and dashed to the Dark Lord and his minions. Muzzles swerved to follow him.

"Your majesty," Ian said, once more forgetting the difficulty people had in understanding him. "This Alandra must be the lady I told you about! That was her! And but for me she would be here!" He turned to the Dark Lord. "She was recaptured by the Norx and taken up by Jat's Pass!"

Lord Kogar's eyes blazed. "You call me a Rat's Ass! Hand the houndson a sword and I'll deal with this challenge."

A squire rushed up, and Ian suddenly found himself holding a weapon. He looked down at it in surprise.

"Defend yourself, vomit spill, so I might have some sport!" Kogar said, grinning as he advanced upon the cobbler's son.

"No!" Hillary cried, running forward desperately. "You idiots, he's trying to tell you where this—"

"One at a time, please!" Kogar said, grabbing the girl and tossing her into the air. Hillary landed hard, moaned once, and was unconscious.

"Bastard!" cried Ian, and before reason could halt him, he moved forward and swung the sword at the lord. The opposing sword leaped up with a flicker-snack and stopped the blow. Ian's weapon almost flew from his grasp. It rang and shuddered as he staggered back.

"By Jove's piss, let's have at it then!" Kogar said, advancing. "I wonder how many pieces I can hack you into in just five seconds!"

"I'm so sorry!" Ian said, suddenly realizing his situation. "I don't want to fight, I just wanted to tell Baron Richard . . ."

"Son of a bitch you call me! I give the names, wretch!" Lord Kogar growled, and he set at Ian, every move that of an experienced fighter.

"Help!" Ian cried. "Please help!" he said, holding up his sword defensively.

"Flea's whelp!" Kogar said. "That's a new one! I shall cut out your tongue and eat it for that one, pig pile!"

Swords clashed and flashed, clanged and rang. The force of the last of Kogar's blows was so great that Ian was shoved backward onto the grass, his breath nearly knocked from him.

A malicious grin making his face like a devil's mask, Kogar moved in for the kill, bringing his sword down hard.

Ian rolled, and the sword slashed off a bit of his clothing. Growling like a maddened bull, the Dark Lord pulled his sword back out of the ground and aimed it for a more accurate strike.

Ian's roll had brought his hand against the pocket that held the cylindrical object. And suddenly that cylinder was in his hand. Reflexively, he raised his hands to protect himself from the coming blow, which fell upon him with all the force that the Dark Lord could muster.

The sword hit the cylinder and snapped in two.

Lord Kogar was thrown off balance, and Ian moved quickly out of the way of another blow. He jumped to his feet, weaving dizzily.

What had happened?

He looked down at the cylinder, astonished, and before he knew what he was doing (as though he had lost control of his hand) he touched the stud at the end of the shaft.

A rapierlike blade shot forth, gleaming thinly in the sun.

"By Balthazar's bats," Lord Kogar cried. "The Pen That Is Mightier Than the Sword."

Seemingly of its own volition, the blade leaped out with dazzling speed and parted Lord Kogar's head from his torso. The head bounced on the ground and rolled toward where Hillary lay. The body staggered about, jetting fluid all over a very surprised Ian Farthing.

Thwippings rushed through the air. The Marines, distracted from their duties by the calamity their leader had met with, suddenly found themselves bristling with arrows. They obliged the Mullshire archers by falling down quite dead.

Knights atop steeds charged the ornithopter and skewered it with their lances. Sparks popped and snapped brilliantly. The machine caught fire and began to burn.

"Nincompoops!" Baron Richard cried. "Oh, now you've brought down calamity upon my head for certain!" He took his glare from the bowmen who had snuck up through the crowd and had been waiting for the chance to let loose their volley, and directed it at Ian Farthing. "And you!" A finger pointed in indignation. "You wretch, what have you done? The Dark Lords will be down my throat within a fortnight! They'll hang us by the heels and flay us alive!"

As Baron Richard Foxshot ranted on, Hillary Muffin awoke and found herself nose to nose with a severed head.

The head opened its eyes and blinked. "By Crom's crumbs, what has happened? I cannot move! Where is my body? What cretin has stolen my body?"

Hillary shrieked and ran to Ian.

"I cut off his head, Hillary," Ian said, wiping the body's fluid from his eyes. "And this isn't blood . . . it's oil of some kind!"

The body referred to took another uncertain step, then flopped onto the ground, spasming violently for a moment, then becoming board-stiff.

The bellowing voice of Lord Kogar stilled the jabber of voices. "A pox upon all your houses! You have put me into a fine fix! Richard Foxshot, approach! I would have words with you!"

Uncertainly, Baron Richard approached the

head, looking as though he were about to bolt. "Lord Kogar . . . this is a most remarkable piece of magic outside the Dark Circle."

"Magic schmagic," Lord Kogar growled. "It's just a mechanical copy of my true body, which lies in a sleeping spell foisted upon me by Lord Morgsteen, who defeated me last year."

"My goodness, I've not kept up with current events very well," Baron Richard said. "But if you're in a sleeping spell . . ."

"Through some mental maneuvering, I managed to invest a mechanical copy of myself with my consciousness, my willpower. It works only intermittently, alas. Damn me, I hate to admit it, but I am sore in need of your help. I should not have played the tyrant about that Alandra bitch. Oh well, I suppose it comes from habit."

"But the flying machine . . ." Baron Richard said.

"Something peculiar happened in the Fabric early yesterday and I had the opportunity to escape with some loyal men and a flying machine. Damned lucky the thing worked in the Dark Circle. Machines seldom do, you know."

"So you're stuck inside that machine head?"

"Alas, yes. My consciousness is at your mercy, I'm afraid."

"No more bluff and bluster?" Baron Richard said.

"Listen here, fellow, I'm a traditional chap,

and as you know, lords have got to have their oratory!"

"I mean, no more threats?"

"Only promises, good Richard. Help me out, and I will ..." The words faded away. The lights in the eyes dimmed. "... communications problem. ..." Sputter. "Hang onto this head ... no football games, hear!"

And then the face stiffened, becoming mask-like.

Baron Richard snapped his fingers. A courtier shuffled up. "Take this thing and place it on a pillow in my antechamber." He turned to Ian and Hillary. "Come with me. We must get you washed up and fed. Apparently we have some talking to do, Ian Farthing. Young lady, I trust you'll ... ah ... interpret." He turned to his subjects and raised his arms and voice. "I trust, good people of Mullshire, that you've had sufficient violence to suit your tastes?"

chapter eleven

ravel across the landscape of the place known as the Dark Circle was at times excruciatingly hazardous, at times breathtakingly awesome, but it was never, never easy. By midafternoon, therefore, the Norx were quite exhausted, having defended Queen Alandra from one hungry dragon, a team of hippogriffs, and a quite lecherous belphagor who clearly cared not a hoot in hell about the importance of Alandra's mythical virginity.

So when Alabaster the cat dropped from the sky directly onto Toothmaw's head, the brutish creature was less than pleased. In fact, his inclination was clearly to hack first and ask questions later.

Frightened witless after its tumble down and down through the Cosmos Corridor, Alabaster clung for dear life atop the noisome head of the Norx. The cat's shriek and the Norx's bellow created quite a caterwaul. Stardust Alabaster had picked up during its fall puffed up and fluttered down, lending the confusion a dense haze of sparkles, which prevented Toothmaw from coming to its fellow's aid.

"It's just a cat!" Alandra cried. "Please don't kill it. It's just scared!"

Toothmaw rid himself of the leather thong connected to Alandra's midriff, and the queen realized that this could be her opportunity to run again. But where to? Besides, the runes had advised her to stay put for the time being, in the interest of her safety and to give whatever Disruption was in the Web-flow a chance to settle.

Tombheart's mount bucked, nearly throwing the thickly bodied Norx from its saddle. Alandra could barely make out the forms in the dazzle-cloud; they were like dancing shadows behind a magical scrim. Tombheart had drawn his sword and was waving it wildly as the panicked feline cavorted wildly about his head and shoulders. It would have been like a comedy, except for the intense fury of it and the clear intent of the Norx to render the cat into dog food. Meanwhile, Toothmaw hovered close by, on his horse, waiting for an opportunity to help.

Suddenly, there was a thunk and a grunt. The cat tumbled from the cloud . . .

. . . landing on its feet, and immediately bounding up to Alandra's horse and leaping into her lap. The poor thing was frosty and shivery and cold, and it huddled against Alandra as though she were its mother.

Tombheart, his sword ringing, weaved for a

moment on his horse, then pitched forward, unconscious, to the ground. The thing had struck himself in the head in his attempt to strike the cat! Toothmaw unhorsed and checked his companion.

"Is he dead?" Alandra asked hopefully.

"No, my lady, only a bruise and a bump," replied Tombheart.

"How can you tell?" Alandra said, clutching the cat closer to herself.

The Norx rose and strode ponderously toward his captive mistress. He held out a hand. "I'll take the beastie and be done with it, madam."

"You'll do nothing of the sort!" Alandra said. "Look, it's doing nothing to harm me! If your idiotic companion had not acted so foolishly, there would have been no problem!"

"A cat that falls from the sky? An evil portent, madam," Toothmaw said, reaching up with his free hand to wrest away the cat.

"You touch me, puke face," said Alabaster, "and I'll slash your heart to ribbons!"

The Norx blinked disconcertedly and snatched away his hand. "A talking cat!" He backed away. "My lady, be done with it. There is a cat that speaks the final words in the Tome of the End Times! We are in a strange era indeed!" Roothmaw's usual rumble actually squeaked with dread.

"Honestly and truly, I really don't talk that much," said the cat. "Please, madam, I've fallen an awfully long way, and more than anything after surviving such a plummet, I should not like to be killed by the likes of that thing!"

Alandra hugged the cat closer. "Of course you won't, my dear! I shan't let them touch you. Have you got a name?"

"I am called Alabaster, my lady, and until recently I was but a simple pet of a magus and I can't really understand what has happened at all and I can tell you right now that I am most dreadfully, awfully, and completely upset at this entire turn of events and—" The cat broke into tears and sobs. "Oh my goodness, I am so very sorry, I am just the most wretched of cats! Tossed out by one's own master! Catastrophe! Ignominy! Perhaps you should just hand me over to the dreadful thing. A quick swipe of that sword and I'll be done with this cruel, cruel multiverse!"

"I'll do nothing of the sort, Alabaster," Alandra said. "I dub you my official pet. You're mine now, kitty, and I'll see that nothing terrible happens to you. We are heading now for my home, where you'll have a nice hearth, and I'll keep your food bowl full, and you'll have a veritable bathtub of fresh milk so that you can grow fat and shiny!"

Alabaster's sobs diminished to purrs as Alandra rubbed its belly. A feline grin appeared on its face.

With a groan, Tombheart rolled over and pushed himself up to a sitting position. "Pain!" he said, rubbing his disgusting head. "Anger! Revenge!" he continued, upon espying the cat

in Alandra's arms. He groped for his sword and
stood, joints creaking horribly. A Norx in a
rage had the tendencies of bulls sighting red
flags; clearly Tombheart was gearing up for a
charge. "Death! Destruction!"

"Trouble!" Alabaster cried, stiffening in Alandra's grasp.

Alandra curled herself defensively around her
new pet. "Toothmaw, don't you think your companion is forgetting himself?" she said coolly
as the maddened Norx raced in for the attack.

Fortunately Toothmaw still had hold of his
faculties; just before the crazed Tombheart could
bring his sword down upon Alabaster, Alandra,
and horse, he stepped in and checked the blow,
with both hands, showing surprising nimble-
ness for a creature of his bulk. He wrestled his
fellow to the ground, then pounded his head
upon a rock until Tombheart's eyes cleared.

Toothmaw stood. "He will be clear-headed
now," the Norx pronounced.

Tombheart rose shakily. "What happened? A
beastie fell from the sky, on my head!"

"I didn't mean to, sir!" Alabaster said. "I
assure you, I had no intention of attacking you,
and the clawing and grasping and such were
pure instinct!"

"You'll not lay a finger on this cat!" Alandra
said regally. "He is a truly wonderful and delightful gift from Heaven itself."

"You shall not keep the thing, my queen,"
said Toothmaw. "Both my brother and myself
agree on this matter. The cat bodes ill!"

"Ill? Now what kind of harm can such a pretty pussycat cause?" Alandra declared, nuzzling her new pet.

"Actually," Alabaster murmured beneath its breath, "you'd be surprised."

"There is nothing you can do about it! Alabaster comes with us, or I shall have your master Morgsteen visit all manner of misfortunes about your head when we reach his palace." She shot them a steely look. "And you know very well the power I can wield over my husband!"

"Very well, my lady," Tombheart said, his voice pure grump and grouch. "But should the beastie cause trouble, it shall either taste my steel, or be cast away."

"It's a deal!" Alabaster said. "Oh, you shall be so happy you have made that fortunate decision, sir! Why, if I care to be, I can sing and dance and tell all manner of delightful tales to dispel the unpleasantness I sense hanging over you all, and I—"

"You shall not speak to me or my brother!" Toothmaw said. "We cannot abide talking beasties. This is my condition!"

Alabaster opened its mouth to say something, then shut it quickly and let a strong nod suffice for answer.

"Well, he can talk to me all he likes!" Alandra said. "I think it's most appropriate and delightful, and it will while away the time!"

"As you wish, my lady!" Tombheart said, clearly not relishing the situation. He turned to his companion. "I like these past two days not at all. We must be on our way, to seek the solace and safety of our master's demesne, praying that he has sent out other of our brothers to intercept us."

They mounted their horses and the journey through the misty, mystical land began again as they picked their way along a riverside, by a darksome forest, from which chirpings and shriekings would emerge, indicating the presence of pixies and sprites and sharp-clawed fangamorphs clearly intent on mischief yet holding themselves at bay at the sight of the powerful Norx and the scent of strong trouble in the air caused by both Alabaster and its new mistress, Queen Alandra.

Alabaster, noting this intuitively, commented, "Crowley Nilrem would say that we stink of magic, mistress. I do not care much for the phrase at all."

"Oh, magic, magic, magic!" Alandra said. "I am heartily sick of magic. Down with sorcery. To hell with necromancy. It's all nothing but a big conglomeration of trouble!"

"Mistress," said the cat, "you speak my sentiments precisely. Why, but for the enchantment of my previous master, God rot his shoe, I should be just a normal housecat, content to eat his fill, bask in the sun, chase mice, and all such manner of delights of finicky predictability housecats enjoy. Instead, cursed with self-awareness by magical manipulation, it is a hard thing to be a cat. Introspection haunts me! And now, I find myself cast out of my delightful home into a strange and frightful land. Oh mistress, I love you much already, but alas I yearn for my comfortable chairs and balls of yarn, my warm hearth and my shadow friends."

"And you shall have all such," Alandra promised, "when these servants of my lord return me to my palace. You shall be happy again, I promise!"

"I do burn with anger at my master," the cat said. "And would have some token revenge, though! I shall pee in his bed! I shall dump my full sandbox in his slippers! I shall claw his finest robes!"

"Your master sounds like every bit the tyrant my husband is," Alandra said. "We are partners in adversity, Alabaster. We shall be good pals indeed!"

"Oh, wonderful, mistress!" said Alabaster. "Oh, I cannot tell you how nice it is to be held and stroked again after the horrific plunge I took! It seemed as though I was falling for ages and ages, past suns and planets and comets and moons. I felt so very small, such a smear in a corridor of night, and now I feel feline again! But mistress, tell me, what is a delightful lady like you doing with a pair of monsters such as these? You say you are in a difficult position. Who are you, and what has happened?"

Alandra, never one to miss a chance to dramatically disgorge her life's story, seized the opportunity immediately and began to narrate.

Alandra Bellworthy was the daughter of King

Leodegrance Bellworthy, ruler of the Primary Quadrant of the Dark Land, last of the Bright Lords. Her mother, according to all sources, had been an angel.

Literally.

"My dear papa always claimed that one night he had the most wonderful dream of his life; the most beautiful woman he had ever seen came to him, declared her love to him, and carried him to a bower of flowers where they were married by fairies, and she made passionate love to him," said Alandra after a rambling beginning to her tale. "He would recall all this to me in a very detailed fashion. He could even name all of the flowers in that bower, and there were many kinds! Of course, he was less descriptive in recalling other aspects of that night. . . . Only he did say that at morning time, although he remembered numerous . . . ah, nocturnal emissions, his sheets were quite dry! And he found feathers. Long feathers! Well, father was always a practical man, positive and constructive. After all, he was a Bright Lord and didn't give much stock to the consequence of dreams, so he just assumed that the feathers escaped somehow from one of his pillows. He put the matter out of his mind completely and absorbed himself in the affairs of his kingdom, namely, how to prevent the Dark Lords from taking over his section of the Circle.

"Then one day, approximately nine months later, he had another dream. In this one, the lady who had wed him returned in a beatific vision. And she had wings . . . an angel of rare glory, holding in her arms a bundle of what at first seemed to be just blankets, but proved to be an infant. 'This is our child, my love,' the angel said. 'I should deign to keep it, but I shall be cast from heaven because of what I have done. Keep her safe and warm.'

"When my father awoke the next morning, he found a baby girl next to him. Me!

"My father, being a bachelor in the eyes of his subjects, naturally was most embarrassed by this state of affairs, and immediately took a wife. Naturally, he could not rid himself of me, for he loved me from first sight. And who, after all, can blame him!"

"Naturally, mistress!" Alabaster said, rapidly learning the importance of performing a chorus function to the queen. "Angelic is the first word that came to mind when I saw you. Which is why I leaped into your caring arms for safety!"

"I was raised as a most beloved princess, and the court magicians were confounded by me. Their divinations from the very beginning showed me to be someone profoundly important, but gradually they began to call me some kind of Key."

"Key, mistress? Your shape is of a soft lovely lady, and you are not cold metal, and the only locks I see are the exquisite ones that crown your head!"

"You are too kind, Alabaster," Alandra said, the cat's words momentarily alleviating her feeling of quite wretched unloveliness. "And that was what I said, in truth as well. I can work no magic, cast no spells! 'Tis true I have my runes, which are the gift of my father through my Treasure Hunt, but they are only devices of consultation and tend to be maddening as often as helpful!"

The stones in the pouch by her side clacked together in annoyed commotion, causing Alabaster to start. "Shut up, you!" Alandra said, smacking the pouch. "Just because I've found someone soft and furry to handle, you are jealous!"

The runes ceased their complaint after a few tiny mutters.

As the sun set, Alandra chatted on merrily about her childhood and early adolescence as a princess, oblivious to the political, magical, and territorial problems that her father was experiencing with his kingdom of Luminos. Once upon a time, ages before, things had been balanced; the Dark Circle had a polarity of power between its four quadrants. But a century before, corruption had taken its toll on Phosphoros, sister quadrant of Luminos. Its Bright Lord had chosen to become a Dark Lord, and the very universe had shaken with the tremors. And then just last year, Morgsteen had finally been victorious in defeating and killing her father, capturing his kingdom, and making Alandra his wife.

"So far, Alabaster, I have kept myself a wife in name only," Alandra said, petting the cat's head thoughtfully. "But after this, I don't know how much longer I can fend off his advances. There is a long stretch of journey before I face that, though. Perhaps I shall be killed in transit and not have to worry about the matter at all!" she said brightly. "So tell me about this magus master of yours that tossed you out, dear Alabaster. I should like to hear something that has absolutely nothing to do with this wretched mess that I find myself in!"

"Mistress," said Alabaster hesitantly. "I am not entirely certainly that that's quite true."

chapter twelve

Ian Farthing had never been in the King's Inner Chambers before. If he had not been stunned and exhausted by the events of the day, he might have been disappointed.

The Throne Hall was large and drafty, with only a few tapestries adding any kind of color to the general gray. The throne itself was just a large wooden chair, carved with symbols, beside a large desk mounded high with records and law books. A pair of whiskered old men, the king's lawyers, sat at one end, looking as though constructed of parchment, ink, and glue themselves. The place smelled of old half-burned logs and extinguished candles and moldy remains of feasts; the baron clearly tended to skimp on housekeeperly affairs.

"Yes yes, well, put it there, put it there," the baron said, tapping one end of the oaken table. "Clear off the dishes first. I don't think Kogar wants the dregs of my breakfast!"

Courtiers obeyed, taking away plates and goblets, placing the tasseled pillow holding the inanimate head of Roth Kogar on the stained wood.

Baron Richard ordered refreshments for his two lower-class guests and instructed them to pull up chairs and sit.

"We shall just have to wait for this thing to come alive again," he said. The baron picked up a cane and tapped the top of the skull. "Anybody in there?" he asked.

No response.

"Now, dear Ian Farthing, town idiot turned champion," Richard said, sitting down and regarding the disheveled, hairy fellow suspiciously. "Just how did you do that?"

Blinking, Hillary turned to Ian as well. "Yes, Ian. How did you do that?"

Ian took out the thing that Kogar had called the Pen Mightier Than the Sword. "I don't know."

"Magic is not supposed to work here in Mullshire . . . well, not any kind of large magic, which that device clearly is! Something is very wrong here!" Baron Richard said, gladly accepting the honey wine a servant had brought, quaffing a great swallow. "Keep it away from me, I tell you that! I'm tempted to confiscate it."

"Oh, please, baron! I should never think of hurting your highness. I had no intention of battling Lord Kogar. It was simply a horrible set of circumstances!"

After listening to Hillary's translation, Baron Richard said, "You cannot blame me for not listening to you before. Your story was quite wild, and from someone of your reputation, Ian Farthing, it was a tale to be laughed at. Apparently, however, its truthfulness has been proved by Lord Kogar himself. As for what it means to us, I truly cannot say!"

"It means, your highness," said Hillary Muffin indignantly, "that we must immediately go to the rescue of this queen in distress!"

"Hillary!" said Ian, feeling slightful doubtful now, and extremely out of his depth. "I think I've had a few second thoughts. . . ."

"Chrmmph . . . cloip . . . hallo!" said the head of Kogar. Intelligence brightened once more in its eyes. "Some kind of interference before. You appear to have moved me. What has happened?"

"That, Lord Kogar," Baron Richard replied noticeably nervous again at the sound of the Dark Lord's commanding bass voice, "is what we hoped you would tell us." He smiled ingratiatingly. "And by the by, welcome, welcome to my Throne Hall."

The Dark Lord's eyes traveled about as far as its stationary position would allow. "What a pigsty!"

The baron was taken aback. "I truly did not expect such august company, Lord Kogar."

"True, true, I did drop in unannounced. I see that the appropriate parties are in attendance. During the break in communication, I have given this matter some thought, and I have a proposal for you. But first, I must submit to you a rendering of the situation as it stands."

Despite the fact that Lord Kogar had a very

short throat, he somehow managed to clear it. Ian was transfixed by the power of the man's oratory. Oh, to speak with such clarity and trilling pronunciation. To savor words like delicate separate morsels of food instead of mounds of Mum's gruel!

"It's quite simple actually," Kogar began. "Several years back I had a wonderful conversation, thanks to the ministry of a pair of splendid Hyperthrifian monks, named Werner and Blowhard, who showed me the error of my Dark and disgusting ways and taught me in two weekends, for a mere pittance, to take responsibility for myself. I made a vow to become a Bright Lord and cease my black designs, thus evening the balance of power in the quadrants of the Dark Circle.

"I found, however, that this would simply not be possible. At least not immediately. For political purposes, namely an uneasy alliance with Lord Morgsteen, I had to continue my bad and blustery evil Act, which explains why I have done all the, ah, questionable things I have done since my Transformation. But be assured, kind friends, within this rough authoritarian persona there beats a kind and gentle heart!"

"Your Act called for you to kill people today with your strong projectile weapons?" Hillary snapped.

"Alas, my previous Evil state has such momentum that occasionally the Act gets carried away and seems to honestly enjoy such violence.

But that is neither here nor there to the present discussion. Now if I may continue!"

Baron Richard glared at Hillary.

"Now where was I? Oh yes! To make a complex tale simplex—or rather, a long story short—I need only say that I was tricked by Lord Morgsteen. Apparently he had discovered my intentions to ally with Lord Luminos, father to Alandra, against him . . . so when he attacked Luminos, he attacked me as well. Fortunately my magic was so strong, he could not kill me. Nonetheless, he put me in the situation that I find myself in now. Fortunately, he does not know about my ability to transfer intelligence to this simulacrum . . . or rather what's left of it.

"So, this is my suggestion. From what you say, gentle people, Queen Alandra has been recaptured by Morgsteen through some bizarre fluke, in which this peculiar specimen of humanity was involved. I know the Dark Land like the back of my paralyzed hand. Gather together a group of knights and together we shall stage a valiant rescue mission! If we can save Alandra from Lord Morgsteen's clutches, you see, we can restore her to her father's throne, and restore harmony to the Dark Circle and the Way Things Are. Splendid idea, eh?"

"I certainly think so!" a brave tenor rang across the chamber like a peal of a crystalline bell. "And Baron Richard," continued the knight known as Sir Godfrey Pinkham, chainmail jingling as he strode across the hall toward the meeting, "with your permission, I should like to lead such a gallant expedition!"

"Pinkham," said the baron, "is it your habit to interrupt important meetings so?"

Sir Godfrey gave a dirty look to Ian and then addressed the baron. "No, my lord, but with all the hubbub, I took the opportunity to consult my astrologist . . . something I was rather remiss about. Indeed, I discovered that yesterday morning I had been scheduled to save a princess, and I presume that the woman that Lord Kogar speaks of, and that Ian Farthing, in his typical fashion, jinxed, is the very lady I was to serve in a chivalrous fashion. Therefore, I should like to claim the right to lead this party of knights into the Dark Circle!"

"And, of course, Ian and I should have to go as well!" Hillary said.

Ian, his stomach doing queasy flip-flops, tugged on her blouse, but before he could whisper in her ear, Lord Kogar recommenced his speech.

"Aye, and wonderful, but beware that no faint heart joins our company. For in the wilds of the Dark Circle there dwell all the evils and dangers ever dreamed of in the imagination of intelligent beings . . . and worse! Humans that venture into its twisted landscape seldom return. Why, I could tell tales . . ."

Ian realized that his legs were beginning to shake uncontrollably.

"But no matter," the Dark Lord continued. "What must be done, must be done. I should speak with the lad who had that weapon that undid me. Where did you find that fabled blade, Ian Farthing?"

"In Merchant's Square, sire!" Ian quavered. "On my way to seek help to rescue the woman you call Alandra."

"Curious. I daresay that we shall have need of it in our journey," Kogar said upon assimilating Hillary's translation. "You, of course, are invited to accompany us, and your little friend to give meaning to your words. I have obtained this feeling about you, Ian Farthing, that—"

"Oh, please, sir," said Ian, his terror unbearable at this point. All of his experiences of the past day, to say nothing of his whole life's record of persecution, suddenly seemed to hang heavy on him. "I should rather not go. I should much prefer to stay in Mull and cobble!"

Hillary turned to Ian, aghast. "But Ian! You must! We must right this terrible wrong. You must make yourself a good name!"

"No!" Ian said, standing from his chair. "No, I have already done all that a poor nothing dunce-lad can possibly be expected to do. I must go now, or my father will use my hide for shoe leather!"

He turned and ran for all he was worth out of the room for home, his heart pounding maniacally.

The young malformed cobbler gave his work his awl.

Pound!

What did they expect of him, anyway, he

thought to himself as he put his hammer down and examined the new hole in the leather by the amber light of a nearby candle. How could they expect the village idiot suddenly to become the village hero? Just because he'd hurled a few lucky blows here and there didn't mean that he was cut out for adventuring, especially across the expanse of a demonic place such as the Dark Circle! No sir, he might be a dunce in the eyes of Mullshire, but Mrs. Farthing didn't raise any idiots!

Now he worked to keep his hands busy, to get his mind off such nonsense! It had all been a dreadful dream, and he had to wake up from it, he told himself, scrabbling about on the worktable to find his cutters. He had work to do, and this was the perfect way to get back into the bleak yet comfortable reality that was his life.

Crip, crip!

Yes, he thought as the scissors cut through the tanned leather and the familiar sounds and sensations of his cubbyhole and his cup of tea wrapped him up like a blanket of security. This is my destiny, and I must hold on to it, for otherwise I shall not only lose my mind, I shall most certainly lose my life!

Not for Ian Farthing the insanity of these past two days! No, better far the misery, squalor, and unhappiness he was familiar with than the terrors and dangers that lurked in the unknown over the border of the Dark Land. At least he had the assurance of a long life here amid all he knew of security, practicing a craft he was competent in, if not exactly excellent! Indeed, there was a wonderful comfort about being merely mediocre. Things were at least predictable here with Mum and Da, if less than exciting.

Ian Farthing had had enough of excitement. He had stumbled somewhere he did not belong, but he had done his very best to right the balance. He'd done his chore, he'd let the outside world know of the plight it was in, and he'd risked his neck sufficiently. How foolish he had been to believe that he might actually participate in Alandra's rescue. . . .

He set down his needle and thread and sighed.

Alandra. She had been so very, very beautiful, tugging at something deep and inexpressible within his soul. He could almost see her beautiful visage now, hear her beautiful voice castigating him for his idiocy. . . .

(*Ian*, a voice seemed to say in his mind. *You can do it, you know you can!*)

"No!" he cried out aloud. "I can't. I'm just the shire simpleton! Anything I touch turns to dross!"

He was working away feverishly at his leathery project when Hillary Muffin found him sometime later.

"You're a daft one, Ian Farthing!" she said, wiping back some strands of her long red hair that had tumbled over her face, then planting her fists indignantly upon her hips. "You come running to me, whining 'bout some beautiful princess whose escape you foiled. Circumstances convince the baron that your tale is true. You show your worth ... and God, I should have liked to see you hack that head off! And now, when you have the opportunity to go out for a quest that will not only help you prove yourself but get you out of this wretched dump of a hovel, you run as though the devil himself were giving you a hotfoot!" She began to pace. "I'll tell you, it was quite mortifying to stand there before the baron and that dreadful Godfrey fellow, to say nothing of that head, while you ran away, leaving a trail of yellow behind you."

Ian did not lift his head from his work to look at her. "What did they say, Hiller?"

"Oh, things about your previous bravery's being an aberration. Truth to tell, they were not surprised. Baron Richard was polite enough to give me something to eat, so I was able to listen to what they plan to do about this situation."

"And what is that, Hillary?" Ian murmured.

"Why do you care?"

Ian shrugged morosely. "Curiosity, I suppose."

"Godfrey Pinkham is tonight selecting a party of six more knights. Seven is a numerologically sound number, apparently. Under the guidance of the head of Lord Kogar, they intend to venture into the Dark Circle tomorrow morning, in hopes of catching up with Queen Alandra and the Norx soldiers who are taking her back to the Palace of Darkshun and her husband Morgsteen. Kogar reports that this is feasible, since the disruption in the Magic Fabric de-

stroyed the Gate through which Alandra escaped, and the party must travel by horse
through the Dark Land, hindered by the many
dangers they will encounter."

"Good," said Ian, reaching for a paste pot.
"You see, Hillary? That's my point. They don't
really need me. In fact, I'd be a hindrance to
them. I can't ride a horse. Never been atop a
saddle in my life, and that sword business . . .
well, as they say, it was just a stroke of luck. Or
desperation, perhaps."

"Ian, Godfrey tried to use that cylinder that
Lord Kogar calls the Pen That Is Mightier Than
the Sword. All he managed to do was to get ink
all over his fingers." She sighed, as though
letting out all of her anger and frustration with
her exhalation. She went to Ian and put her
arm around his shoulders and leaned her head
against his. "Oh, Ian, can't you understand?
All of my life I've seen things in you—wonderful things—and suddenly, in the past two days
you're beginning to show others that you're not
a simpleton, you are Someone, and Someone
Very Special! And suddenly, you act just as
they expect you to act."

"That's because that's the way I am," Ian
said, pushing Hillary's arm away from him.
"That's the way I want to be, Hillary. It's . . .
it's safe! I don't want to die! You don't know
what all this has been like for me. It's not
exciting, it's scary." He turned to her and stared
into her eyes entreatingly. "Hillary, it's like I'm
standing on a precipice and all that's before me

is a darkness and Void . . . and you're bloody well screaming at me to jump into it. There's nothing but dead bodies at the bottom of such, Hillary, and though they may call me one, I am truly no fool. At least, not that kind of fool."

"But don't you see, Ian? That's the way life should be lived!"

"Jumping off cliffs? Not much life there!"

"No, you're right, Ian, and it is scary. I had a wise old gypsy grandmother and she told me many tales and much wisdom—"

"Oh yes, and fiddlesticks to her. I've heard more than my share of tales and I—"

"Would you listen to me, Ian Farthing?" Hillary said furiously. "I have never before encountered anyone so stubborn! Now, as I was saying, my grandmother always said that a life lived well was always new, that the past and the future were just illusions, and that the present, when we see it right, is always a leap into this Void you've been talking about, that we just have to do what seems right . . . and that action will take us where we're supposed to go! Ian, we have to be open to the opportunities that are given us! And oh dear Ian, this is your opportunity."

"Opportunity to die, opportunity maybe even to lose my immortal soul!" Ian threw his work back onto the table. "Hillary, haven't you heard the tales about the demons and the awful things that dwell in the Dark Circle, who hunger to carry your soul into Eternal Perdition? No, I'm not so foolish as to go there, Hillary! No, I shall

live a good Christian life here in Mullshire,
and I shall do the duties that society demands
of me, and then I shall reap my reward in
Heaven, which sounds like a much more pleasant, safer place to be!"

"Ian, this is not you speaking!" Hillary said.
"This not the Ian with the head full of plans
and dreams, of imagination and of hope! Ian, I
believe in you! Why can't you believe in yourself, now that you have the chance to prove to
yourself what you are?"

Ian Farthing turned away, stifling a sob. "I
. . . oh, Hillary, I just can't." He began to tremble.

"Now don't have one of your fits, Ian! You're
just trying to escape yourself, run away from
what you really are and can really do!"

She grabbed him by the face and turned his
head toward hers.

"I love you, Ian Farthing. There is so much
that is good and true and right inside of you!
There is so much potential for a kind of good
that only dwells in legends. All I ask of you
now is that you believe in yourself, that you
love yourself, that you don't settle upon that
stubborn attitude that others have foisted upon
you and instead, take the chance to find out
who you really are! Haven't you ever wondered where you really came from, why the
Farthings found you wandering in this town,
an outcast from somewhere? Ian, this is the
chance for you to find out. I can feel it. All the
answers to the questions you've hardly dared
ask are over that border! Ian, I love you. Please

love yourself enough to take a chance on yourself. This may be the last opportunity."

Shivering, Ian turned away, placed his arms around his head, and began to shiver and sob. "Please ... please leave me, Hillary. Just go. I can't take this."

"They are leaving in the morning, Ian," Hillary said after a moment of silence. "Please think about what I've said, and consider what you might be losing by not doing what you know you must do."

She left him.

Ian Farthing had never felt so alone and empty and wretched in the entirety of his alone, empty, wretched days.

"No!" he said, picking up his work. "She can say what she pleases, but I am a survivor, and this is the best place to do that!"

He looked around for the sole he had cut to make this shoe complete ... but it was nowhere to be found.

chapter thirteen

"There it is!" said Crowley Nilrem, precariously perched upon the top of the ladder. A fine spray of plaster filtered down upon his head as he reached for the thick volume on a top library shelf. Nilrem looked up, noting with chagrin the new series of crazes in the ceiling. His precious mansion was a network of cracks now. His expulsion of Alabaster had slowed the crumbling deterioration considerably, but had not stopped it entirely. Other desperate measures were needed. This was why the magus needed the leather-bound volume marked with all manner of gold-embossed cuneiforms.

The ladder tilted for a moment; Nilrem teetered at the top, panicking for only an instant, recovering handily with a screeched balance spell in pidgin Elvish, roughly translatable as "Not while I have a will/Will I go for a spill!"

The magus descended the ladder carefully step by creaky step, when repaired for the Gaming Room, where the Book of Roles could be utilized most effectively, where the Rolling Magic was centered.

He had never before had to resort to this dread tome, holding secrets terrible, secrets primal, resonant of the very underlying nature of Existence, mostly because the spells utilized were so damned unpredictable. He'd heard stories, though, from others of the Nine, about sorcerers who had used the Book of Roles unwisely, and been blasted to cinders by unmentionable demons from the darkest pits of alien hells. The usual Games of the Nine were much safer, since the Eldritch Manses were sufficiently removed, as it were, from the refracted playing fields of the symbols and archetypes they manipulated. However, whatever the disruption Alabaster had caused, (or from the looks of it now, that had caused Alabaster's gaffe), it had Crowley Nilrem's manse in its grip, and the only way that Nilrem knew of making things right, short of an Emergency Assembly of the Nine (which would be an extreme embarrassment and cause him to lose points in the End Tally), was to resort to the Roles.

"Primal magic, indeed," he murmured under his breath, looking at the Destiny Board as he entered. Kogar and his flying machine were in Mullshire, and the pieces had all fallen on their faces. Goodness alone knew what that meant. His eyes turned to the Norx pieces with their captive queen, and he gasped.

There was a new piece to the party, a cat.

"Alabaster?" Nilrem said, pulling at his side-boards in vexation. "Oh, dear, dear, dear. The power emanated by Alandra must have attracted the poor beast in its tumble. Well, I haven't the foggiest what the significance of this is, but at least they will both have pleasant company for a time!"

Crowley Nilrem's feelings on the subject were rather vague, because ever since the Disruption, Crowley Nilrem himself was rather vague. Every few minutes he fancied that a bit of him was missing, which was a curious sensation, as yet unsubstantiated by actual material loss of hands or nose or feet, but nonetheless trouble-some particularly when matters of memory or character arose. Nilrem had always prided him-self on a rock-solid Games Magician character, consisting of fortitude and perseverance, to say nothing of fascination with strategy and the rules of chance, underscored by other worthy attributes. But now, in this time of crisis, his absentminded, abstract nature was coming to the forefront.

In fact, the magus was a mess.

His neat Victorian-gentleman facade seemed to disintegrate in harmony with his Victorian mansion. His tie was undone, his hair and whiskers ratty. His previously shiny Oxfords were scraped and scuffed, his shirt hung out, and there were holes in his pants.

He felt as though he were coming apart.

He poured himself a large measure of brandy and drank a gulp to settle his nerves, then opened the thick book and sneezed. Dust plumed up. Crowley Nilrem plucked out a handkerchief, wiped his nose, then swept some of the dust off the vellum pages with the linen cloth.

The book was done in the tiresome old medieval style practiced by bored monks with nothing better to do, elaborately inked Latin, colored illuminations, and all. Crowley Nilrem sighed, trying to dredge up his memory of dead languages, and commenced to read.

Some minutes and a few pages later, he had a grasp of what he had to do.

"Crowley Nilrem, alchemist!" he murmured unhappily. "Science of the Stoned Philosophers! Dross into gold indeed!"

But this bit of alchemy had nothing to do with stones or philosophy or for that matter gold, but a simple alchemical preparation mixed up with a mortar and pestle.

Bat's tongue, worm dung; squid spit, pixie shit: of course, Crowley the magus had them all, along with the necessary mercury and sulfur, and other less savory chemical compositions vital to an alchemist's kit. After combining the oddments, he mashed the odoriferous conglomerate and heated it beneath a Bunsen burner. The dry residue was then spooned out into little piles upon the seats of chairs set around the Gaming Table.

Crowley Nilrem consulted the Book of Roles once more for the final instruction, and grimaced.

He needed a razor blade. But why a rusty razor blade? Well, no time to question.

He rooted around his drawer of sharp-edged tools and came up with a true gem of a razor, once used by a village barber to shave, cut hair, let blood, and perform public executions. A truly multipurpose instrument, centuries ahead of its time, this blade was suitably rusty, with a bonus spatter of blood that the Necromancers' Exchange had charged him extra for. Generally this kind of barbaric (or perhaps barberic) measure was not called for in his usual line of gaming enchantments. However, times were desperate; this kind of hazard was something a Gaming Magus had to expect if he was to truly succeed at his delicate and chancy craft.

Nilrem had set out five extra chairs around the table. He hovered over the first one and intoned his spell. "That the role I play now is perfection/bring up another for resurrection./ That I might complete my destined Task/ Bring forth a segment of my mask."

He groaned with pain and distaste as he cut his finger and let some of the blood drop onto the alchemical mixture. He repeated this on each seat, squeezing drops of blood like punctuation to his spell. When each seat had its portion of blood and dust, he sat at the head of the table and drew a pentagram on his forehead with his own blood.

"That I may reach my appointed goals," he said in Latin, "bring forth the shades of my five roles!"

A deafening thunder cracked within the room, and Nilrem muttered under his breath. This primal stuff was much too dramatic, he thought, as bolts of lightning slashed from nowhere, touching the chairs, illumining them in spectral glow.

For a moment, the room dropped into complete darkness; and then the lights magically reignited.

Nilrem blinked with surprise, even though he knew exactly what to expect. Still, it was difficult to come face to phase with himself!

Face to phases, rather.

Five of his previous personae in the Great Game sat around the table now, astonished expressions plain on their countenances. Five of the most important characters the being calling himself Crowley Nilrem had played to ascend the levels toward magushood.

Crowley Nilrem blanched at these sudden apparitions. How awfully unsubtle this method was! He realized that he had progressed so far up the line that he had lost his taste for the common aspects of the Game, losing himself instead in its delicacies and nuances.

He recognized his warrior self, young, dumb, and full of rum, complete with broadsword and beard, dagger and swagger. Nilrem cringed. Smell, too.

Then there was the cleric, telling his talisman rosary; and the dwarf; and the elf; and lastly, on the opposite side of him, was the monk, face concealed by a large hood.

"Please, do not be excited," Crowley Nilrem said. "You are in friendly territory and I have to use you only a short time."

"Ah!" said the warrior, his breath smelling of garlic. "An adventure. Plunder and blunder. Rape and pillage!"

"Good heavens, why must every one of these foolish games be supplied with someone of his ilk?" his cleric self complained. "I take it you are a mighty wizard, about to assign us to some task that we might grow in power and holiness?"

"Not precisely, my friend," Nilrem said. "I assure you that your journey has a most successful conclusion. No, let us merely say that I have use of you all to help me with that most necessary of all elements to the Game Player's attributes. Not strength, nor dexterity. Not armor, nor resistance to spells. No, I speak of willpower, and you must all help me to restore mine, by uniting yours into one matrix."

"How dreadfully banal!" chirped his elf self. "Can't we chase after some kind of magical ring? I quite enjoy that sort of thing. I met this philology professor once who would have been a wonderful gamemaster! Suppose he's underground by now, but then, what's a little death between a necromancer and a corpse? What do you say, oh sorcerous summoner?"

"Oh, you know his type," the dwarf said in a cockney accent. "Probably has magic rings up the wazoo. Besides, those kinds of quests are always Mordor. Arr, arr." The dwarf speared the magus with a piercing gaze. "Say, mate, speaking of rings, I don't suppose in your magical surveys of things you've spotted a chap named Siegfried, did you? My ax would like a little heart-to-heart with old Siegfried, it would."

"Please, gentlefolk," the magus said, realizing, of course, that by the very nature of the Game, these characters would have no idea that he, Crowley Nilrem, Gaming Magician extraordinaire, was the culmination of them all. "Weapons will not be necessary for this little affair."

"Well then, how about a drink?" the warrior demanded. "These blasted wizards have been getting bloody cheap lately. Can't even offer an honest pint of ale."

"Oh, very well," Crowley Nilrem said, getting up and bringing a tray of decanters over to his guests. He'd forgotten; practically all his previous characters had a taste for drink, an unfortunate quality that had landed them in no end of trouble.

"Ta, mate!" said the dwarf, snagging the schnapps, not bothering to avail himself of a glass. "Always first accursed with a thirst, that's me."

"So then, wizard," the monk said from beneath his cowl after pouring himself some Pernod. "Repeat again your name and the task you would have us perform."

"My name is Crowley Nilrem," the magus said. "I simply wish, with your aid, to form a paradigm reflecting myself and the present situation in which I find myself and this continuum." He gestured at the board. "This is the level presently under scrutiny. It was at this level that the trouble began and the trouble continues."

"Cor blimey!" the dwarf said. "I recognize that place! That's the bloody Dark Circle. I've already lost me share of points—to say nothing of blood—in that accursed place."

The elf too seemed chagrined. "The Dark Circle is the garbage pit of imagination! Why, I've never seen so many different magics, races, and mythologies crammed into one stretch of land. I certainly don't intend to venture again into that place!"

"No, no," said Crowley Nilrem. "You misunderstand. There is no reason to actually physically enter the Circle. All I ask is a primal source gaming ritual amongst us all—The Rite of the Roles."

"Well, why didn't you say so?" the cleric said, smiling. He put away his rosary, jammed a hand into his pocket, and pulled out a handful of many-colored dice, which clacked onto the bare wood. "Always ready for a roll in the—hey! I'm missing my big sixty-four-sided die!"

"Only traditional six are necessary, my friend," said Crowley Nilrem.

"Boring, boring, boring," said the warrior. "I cannot imagine anything so dull. I graduated from all that, fellow! Now I really get to swash some buckle and explore uncensored adventure. Thud and blunder forever!"

"Humor me, please," said Crowley Nilrem.

"This is for all our sakes, and will take only a short time!"

"Shakin' the ivories is all right by me, mate," said the dwarf, "but what's in it for us?"

"Yes!" said the elf, putting an arm around the gnarled, hairy little man. "An excellent question from my esteemed colleague."

"Get your paws off me, you bleedin' fairy!" the dwarf demanded.

Instantly the dwarf found a point of dagger under his chin. "I've always favored barring the dim-brained dwarvish types from serious Games, sausage-breath. Shall I start my campaign with you?"

"Please, please," Nilrem cried. "You would only be cutting your own throat. Oh goodness, clearly I am a macropsychologist's dream!"

The elf put away his dagger under protest, and they all began to sort out their dice for the necessary steps of the ritual.

All, except for the monk, who sat in his place, his hands wrapped together solemnly, his Pernod untouched.

"Good monk," said Crowley Nilrem, "you have been formally invited to play. By the code of the Gamer you must participate. I ask only a small part of your time, after all. Would you begrudge me so little?"

"Right, mate! Let's get the show on the roll! Stop monking around!" the dwarf said. He picked up a cube of ivory and brandished it. "Do or die, that's my motto!"

"Does our new companion have religious scruples perhaps?" the elf ventured. "Would a prayer improve his mood?"

"I make a habit," said the monk, reaching up for his cowl, "of praying only to myself"

"Arr harr!" the dwarf said. "Don't you know! Idol hands are the devil's playthings!"

"I agree with the warrior," the monk said. "This is quite boring. I think we should change things considerably."

The monk threw back his cowl.

The others gasped.

Crowley Nilrem said, "Oh goodness. No wonder . . ."

Where there should have been a head, perhaps with a cap, was a ball of shimmering stars. Comets orbited this cluster like electrons in an atom, glowing with a power that throbbed into the soul of the observer. Within this blazing mass, the faint outlines of a face could be seen.

"Change is, of course, only the aspect of the multiverse that is constant," the creature said. "From time to time, should not the constant itself be changed?"

"Why have you returned?" Nilrem demanded. "Things were working well!"

"Of course they were! Perhaps I grow bored. Perhaps I seek revenge. Perhaps I fulfill my destiny. Perhaps I am a mere victim of some obscure prophecy. And then again, perhaps I am not who you think! Choose one of the above, Crowley Nilrem."

Nilrem panicked. "Personae! This Game of

Roles is not what I thought it would be! Kill him! Treasure and points will be yours beyond your wildest dreams! There are levels in the universe beyond your imagination! Kill this thing, and you will ascend to paradise."

"One swipe will punch out your lights, pal!" said the warrior. His muscles swelled as he lifted his broadsword.

"I believe this star has your name on it, barbarian," said the creature, plucking a speck from his countenance. "Would you care to look more closely?" The star was tossed. It drilled straight through the space between the warrior's eyes. The man dropped dead onto the floor, then discorporated back into the alchemical ash he had arisen from.

Nilrem jerked with pain.

"A clear case of burnout, wouldn't you say, Crowley?" said the apparition. "I believe I've a few more to spare for all of you!"

With amazing speed, the others charged their nemesis, but were easily dispatched with flung stars and reduced back to powder mixed with Nilrem's dried blood.

Crowley Nilrem gasped with each blow to his persona.

"You are toying!" he said.

"You may perceive it as such, magus," said the creature. "But you should know by now that everything has a reason."

"I must stop you!" Nilrem said, but he found that he could not rise.

The starry head leaned closer to the Gaming

Board. "An interesting situation, but much too traditional, don't you think? I mean, Crowley, dragons and centaurs and dwarves and wizards and knights and barbarians and princesses are all very nice and archetypal. But a dash of the new is necessary, I think." The map began to float up. "Perhaps things need to be turned topsy-turvy just a teensy bit!" The board turned over, but the playing pieces remained in place. "A little more, perhaps." Suddenly, the board separated and reconnected in the form of a Moebius strip. It began to glow and change colors like a barber's pole dipped in a rainbow. It hovered in the air, surrounded by some kind of scintillating field of force.

"I shall spare you now, Nilrem," said the starry-headed creature. "Because I need you. Go before the Nine. All of you must work together for me if you value your lives. I shall return to you again. I think that between the lot of you, my needs can be divined. I expect them to be met by the time of my return!"

In a blaze of light, the robed creature disappeared.

The Gaming Board remained in its position, turning slowly like a mobile hung from the ceiling by an invisible thread. The dice his blasted personae had left dangled midair in various positions about the Moebius-strip map like gamblers' moons.

The magus felt his strength returning slowly.

He poured himself a drink, then pulled an antique phone from a cabinet.

He dialed 9 to get out.

"Yes?" a voice answered.

"Mother!" said Crowley Nilrem, gazing in horror at the new configuration of the Gaming Board.

chapter fourteen

The dawn cracked.

In fact, it cracked in several places, fissures zigzagging from pink-touched mountainous horizon to where the sky was still dark.

For Alandra and Alabaster and their guardian (or rather, captor) Norx, the cracking was quite spectacular, as well as being so noisy it woke the sleepers up.

"Earthquake!" Alabaster screeched as the ground trembled.

"Skyquake!" Alandra said, watching the sky tearing into pieces.

"Stomachquake!" said Toothmaw, wretching with motion sickness.

The cat and the queen leaped for each other, holding on tight, bouncing about in the blankets.

Tombheart grabbed the horses so that they would not run away. Mighty winds gusted, sweeping across the clearing, bending the trees in the forest double.

Great lights and dazzles like stars gone mad leaked through the rents in the sky, mixing with the torrent and howling like lost souls.

As though invisible scissors were at work, the tears in the sky began to move across the landscape, tearing the land in two.

The party and their horses headed for Dark-shun were shaken back into senselessness.

The entirety of the Dark Circle was in a tumult, ripping and twisting out of shape. A haze of dust dimmed the sun, casting a kind of grim twilight upon the ensorceled land.

Sir Godfrey Pinkham coughed from the dust and ordered his men to dismount and take cover.

"God's wounds!" he cried as he secured his terrified horse to a tree. "We've only just started! We haven't reached the borders of the Dark Circle yet!"

The ground began to sway beneath the knight's wobbly knees. Desperately, he untied the shiny walnut box that held the head of their guide, flipped off the latch, and opened it. "Lord Kogar!" Pinkham screamed. "What is happening?"

But the eyes refused to open and the mouth did not answer.

A gigantic boom, like grounded thunder, swept all thoughts from the knight's head. A gust of wind banged him against the tree and he lost consciousness.

This gray twilight spewing from cracked dawn flowed like a rushing river over the town of Mullshire, twinkling in places with the detritus of the Dark Land's magic.

Ian Farthing, huddled in his blankets and

uneasy dreams, was awakened by the seemingly distant commotion. He groggily peered up from his bed at the shuttered window, and noted that only darkness seeped through the cracks.

Needing nothing violent to encourage him, Ian Farthing turned over and surrendered his consciousness to sleep.

Hank the knacker awoke to the sounds of distant weathery turmoil. It was not the clash of thunder nor the sear of lightning nor the rush of wind that awoke him, but rather a clatter at his gate, and anxious barking.

For the love of God, thought Hank. It sounds like ole Night's come back.

"Oooh!" he said as he rolled from his blankets, bedclothes tousled, and searched for his slippers. What a head he had! Too much drink yesterday.

The bark came again, followed by an anxious scratching at wood.

"Bah!" he said, giving up the search. "Hold ye, ole Night! I'll be with ye by and by."

His belly rumbled. He burped, tasting the foul remains of yesterday's feasting and drinking. "I'll just let Night in and then visit the old mattress again for a few more winks," he promised himself. "I deserve it, I do!"

It was only when he reached his yard, out in the open, that Hank the knacker realized that there was something wrong.

"Good Lord," he said, looking up into the

sky. "It wasn't the ale and the mead that gave those fairy dreams!"

The sky was a chiaroscuro of color, filled with fleeting half-seen forms, weird shapes. Edges of clouds seemed on fire, whipped into crimson froth by the wind. The sun could be barely seen, surrounded by a corona of dust.

"What is going on?" he said. There was something weird in the air, a taste of dread, a smell of magic that Hank the knacker had experienced only at the fringe of the—

"Jesus, Mary, and Joey," he whispered. "Has the bleedin' Circle busted a gut?"

He stubbed a toe on a pot, tripped, and almost tumbled into a caldron of animal fat ready to be boiled into tallow today. Yesterday's collection of dead cats and dogs lay in a pile by the workbench, patiently awaiting their turn to be skinned. Hank righted himself and forged onward along the path made through stacks of animal fur, bottles, pans, and other knacker knickknacks.

Hank sniffed. Something was wrong here in his yard. Where was the comforting odor of decay, the delicate musks of death? Was there something wrong with his nose?

The scratching again. He'd let Night in, then go back into his house, get out his casket of crosses and talismans, and cover himself in their protection beneath the covers of his bed. Something was awfully wrong in Mullshire, and he hoped it would blow over, quickly.

Hank reached the gate and put a hand on the latch, halting a moment. "Night? That you, son?"

A bark answered his question.

"Right. We'll have you inside in no time!" Hank the knacker said, undoing the latch and opening the door. "There's a good dog! Where, for the love of God, 'ave you—"

Standing in front of him, balanced on two paws, was half a dog.

"Hallo, Hank," said Night, teeth shiny through an attempted canine smile.

"What happened? And you're talkin'!"

"Actually, who's talking is not your dog, but a spirit presently animating its remains for a time. It's a great trick. Wonderful fun! I shall enjoy showing it to all of you Mullshire folk now that things have changed, and there's more territory to explore. Just flowing along on this beast's instincts for now, actually, savoring its memories. Why, look at that lot over here. . . ." Hank watched in horror as the half-dog walked toward the pile of dead cats and dogs in the knacker's yard. "Yo ho. Fun, fun, fun!"

"Who . . ." said Hank. "Who . . . how . . ."

"Chap by the name of Ian Farthing started it all, to tell you the truth. Even got your dog Night killed. You may well ask, Hank, how a mere spirit can do what I do, and I can only answer: elementally, my dear chap!"

The eyes of a dead cat shot open. A dog rolled over and growled. One by one, like newborn pet zombies, the creatures in the pile creaked into life.

"Hello, my new friends," said the puppet-master spirit. "Let us go and roam the streets of our lovely new town. Let us chase rats and mice in joy! Let us welcome dark magic into the land of Mullshire."

Hank the knacker ran for his life.

chapter fifteen

"Alandra!" a small voice called in her ear. "Wake up, mistress! Oh, please don't be dead!"

Alandra raised her head groggily, silky hair spilling into her face. "Dead? I'm dead? It could only be a change for the better." She felt the tickle of Alabaster's whiskers, and then she remembered the upheaval in the sky and in the ground. "Alabaster, what happened?"

"Mistress," said Alabaster, "the scientists and sorcerers of this land believe that this world is round. They are wrong. It is quite flat, with squared edges. I know . . . I have seen representations of it in appropriate perspective."

"I asked you what happened, Alabaster," Alandra said, peering about dizzily, unable to make out much. She rubbed her eyes. "I did not ask for a lesson in geography."

"Mistress, geography has gone quite gaga. This entire world seems to have changed in shape from flat to . . . well, apparently connected strips. My eyes can see better than yours."

"I'll take your word, Alabaster. Where are the Norx?" she said.

"Here, oh queen," responded Tombheart. "We are calming the horses."

"We are lucky to yet be alive! Truly majestic sorcery has today been at work!" said Toothmaw. "The horizons have changed!"

The dust in the sky had abated somewhat, and Alandra could tell that the Norx and Alabaster spoke the truth. When she looked up, instead of clouds she could see land coiling away into the sky like a crazy-quilt coiling. The sun was just beginning to peek around one side of the bizarrely skewed horizon, washing away a dark shadow cast across this section of the terrain.

"Perhaps," Alandra said meekly, "I should have stayed with Morgsteen after all."

"All is lost," groaned Toothmaw. He glared at Queen Alandra. "Brother, a sacrifice is in order to appease the gods!"

"A pleasant thought," said Tombheart, "but you forget, brother, our sacred vows to Morgsteen. Our mission is to bring him back his wife, not kill her."

Toothmaw grumbled, but agreed. "But which way do we go? Between us and Morgsteen's palace may lie an uncrossable chasm now!"

"We can only travel, brother, and see what awaits us." He swung his heavy, ugly face toward Alandra. "Prepare to mount, oh queen. A long and weird journey indeed awaits us."

"I must consult my runes!" Alandra said adamantly.

"Consult them at your leisure atop your steed!" the Norx growled fearsomely. "And give us no more of your tongue, lest we do the right thing and make a sacrifice of you!"

"Imaginative fellow," said Alabaster.

"Alabaster, do you think your former master, Crowley Nilrem, the one who cast you out, had something to do with this?"

"I cannot see how he cannot be unaware of an event of this magnitude . . . but mistress, truly, he has not the power to actually cause it. No, mistress, as our captors say, majestic power indeed is afoot!"

"Well, that foot must have kicked damned hard to do something like this," said Alandra, gazing up in wonder at this frightening new world about her.

In the life of Godfrey Pinkham, there had never been any doubt as to what course his destiny would take. Born of noble blood—his father a cousin to the Foxshot line, his mother descended from the One King Himself—the lad had been born with, if not a silver spoon in his mouth, then something very much like it. His early youth, when not abusing younger, less well-nourished serfs, was spent imagining the glories of that fabled destiny: knighthood! He dueled with wooden swords, lanced all manner of wiggling worms and grotesque gryphons, and, naturally, saved damosels in distress—a rigorously channeled form of imagination he had not the imagination to question. With prepubescence, he became a page, where he learned the more refined elements of chivalry and manners from the most delicate and beauteous of ladies, practicing their needlepoint ways in the tapestry of courtly life. With adolescence, he graduated to an apprenticeship as a squire, eased roughly into the manly rites of chainmail and swordplay, muscling his way vigorously through the tide of human endeavor as an aid to a seasoned knight. Finally, at the age of nineteen, when he could bash and slash with the very best, Godfrey was dubbed Sir Godfrey by the baron himself in a glorious ceremony where he felt an ecstasy just short of a Galahad-type vision of seraphim, cherubim, and God Himself.

Then, for the next few years, absolutely nothing happened. No wars, no quests, no damosels in distress; only the odd tournament to prove his prowess.

Sir Godfrey grew bored.

It was during this time that a gypsy had read his Tarot and pronounced that somewhere in the handsome knight's future there indeed was a beautiful damosel to be saved, and a very important damosel at that, whose saving would earn Godfrey unimaginable glory and renown.

So it was quite natural that when word of the plight of Princess Alandra reached him, he employed every amount of his political power to secure the position of Head Savior of the party sent into the Dark Land under the direction of the Dark Lord Kogar's mechanical head. Equally

natural was the knight's consternation and chagrin when catastrophe struck even before one
horse hoof was placed over the Dread Border.

"Damn!" was his first word upon reawakening
to find his party of seven a shambles about
him. "What has happened?"

Godfrey Pinkham's world view was a fairly
well-ordered one, so the restructured shape of
the terrain—landscape for wall and ceiling—was
a sizable shock upon the knight's sensibilities.

"Zounds," he cried. "Black sorcery at its most
heinous!" He took a deep breath and closed his
eyes to recover from the dizziness that swarmed
about him. "We must recover this queen! Already the promised catastrophes are occurring!"

He went from knight to prostrate knight, waking them up, helping to reorient them, urging
them onward.

"There had better be plenty of riches and
glory in all of this!" grumped Sir Oscar Cornwall as he remounted his steed.

Frightened agreement from the others greeted
his words. Godfrey suspected that only knightly
momentum kept them from turning tail and
running back home to wife and mother.

"Can't you see?" said Sir Godfrey. "This quest
will be the stuff from which the greatest legends will be made!" Despite his grandiose
statement, however, he could not help but allow a quiver of uncertainty to infect his voice.

"Aye," said Sir Ronald Komquatte. "But what
good are legends to us when we are dead?"

"We have our duty, gentlemen," said Sir
Godfrey. "Our duty is sacred."

None of the knights could disagree with that; the notion was as much a part of them as their flesh or blood.

"Perhaps that chap Kogar has a word or two of explanation and advice," Sir Mallory suggested.

"He was uncommunicative at the time of disruption," Sir Godfrey said. "But I shall try again."

The walnut box had fallen onto the ground. Sir Godfrey picked it up and opened the latch.

The head's eyes were wide open.

"Something quite ludicrously awful has happened," Lord Kogar said. "Even under my paralysis spell in my castle, I can feel it."

"Your intuitions are quite correct, Lord Kogar," said Godfrey, holding up the head so that it could have a good view of the new set of surroundings. "Have a look!"

The mechanical eyes made of glass lenses surveyed the curled horizons and the mechanical mouth frowned. "I confess," the head said finally, "I am out of my depth. This reconfiguration is . . . unprecedented."

"Have you any idea at all as to its meaning and portents?" asked Sir Oscar Cornwall.

"No," said Lord Kogar, after a moment's thought. "Some sort of essential shift has occurred in the structure of things."

"We had not noticed!" said Sir Mortimer Shieldson, voice muffled as usual by his thick drooping mustache.

"By Neptune's nostrils, I can do without

sarcasm!" Lord Kogar exclaimed, back to his overbearing self.

"Does this have something to do with Queen Alandra?" asked Godfrey, gesturing toward the changed land.

"No, no, something more is happening," Lord Kogar growled. "Something of which . . . could it be? Have I been concentrating so much on Alandra and the polarity of the quadrants, to say nothing of Morgsteen's plans, that I have forgotten? Oh, for the use of a good astrologist specializing in eschatology now!"

"What are you speaking of, Lord Kogar?"

"Pay my wandering mind no heed, Sir Godfrey."

"Has our quest lost its meaning?" asked Sir Ronald, hopefully eyeing the path back.

"By Jupiter's toenails, of course not! If anything, it has gained in profundity! And if you value the welfare of your insignificant little land, your smelly little village, you'll press onward, under my direction!"

"But surely, Lord Kogar," said Sir Oscar, "if things are so different, how will you know the way to Morgsteen's palace . . . or, indeed, if that establishment exists now at all?"

"Fear not, I can still direct your ways. Let us hope, Sir Doubtful, that we catch up with Queen Alandra before the Norx carry her all the way back to her unspeakable hubby's establishment!"

"Did you hear that, men?" Sir Godfrey bellowed, reaffirming his authority over the group. "Remount, and proceed on our course!" He turned back to face the face in the box. "I shall keep you out. We approach the border, and we shall need your advice every step of the way."

Lord Kogar agreed that this was an excellent idea. Sir Godfrey took him from the box and held him under one arm as they rode.

The separation between the outside and inside of the Dark Circle was much less distinguishable now; indeed, Sir Godfrey noted as they rode on, the dusky atmosphere seemed charged now with a different feel. Even the trees seemed somehow more bent, more sinister.

He commented on this to the head beneath his arm.

"Yes, yes, somehow the magical atmosphere has overrun the boundaries," Lord Kogar said, after a survey. "This I like not at all. Magic should be kept in its place. This denotes a terrible change in the balance of the very cosmos, Godfrey. This particular quest you are on is much more vital than you can ever imagine."

Sir Godfrey nodded seriously. "I understand. Be assured that we have here the very finest knights of Mullshire."

"It is too bad that the twisted, ugly fellow who beheaded me elected not to travel with us."

"Who, Ian Farthing? He is but the town idiot. His victory over you was mere happenstance. Besides, we have the weapon he used for our purposes. What use, Lord Kogar, would we have for a simpering simpleton?"

"I disagree with you. There is something about

the fellow, perhaps akin to the situation in which we find ourselves. In foolish times, what better friends than full-time fools?"

"You play with words, Lord Kogar," admonished Sir Godfrey. "He would be nothing more than a hindrance, not even good for entertainment value. Believe me, I have known of the clod for many years. His actions preventing the successful escape of Queen Alandra were surely a harbinger of things to come. This is a time for heroes with steel tongues and great hearts, not twisted gnomes."

"We shall see," said Lord Kogar. "We shall see, my dear Sir Godfrey."

They traveled on toward darker, craggier parts, the smell of grim autumn heavy in the spring air.

For the first time in his life, Sir Godfrey Pinkham was uncertain. As he looked at the warped horizon, he wondered if he was truly on a mission of glory and honor, and not one of potential death and failure. Things had happened in just the past twenty-four hours that gave the young man a different viewpoint on life. Could it be, after all, that his valor, his bravery, and his accomplishments would not be the center about which the universe spun?

No, he thought, cheering up immensely.

Why, surely all this was just a test from God Himself, to see if Godfrey should ascend upon his death to the very highest levels of heaven, rather than merely to the usual lofty place reserved for brave knights.

Do your worst, Satan, he thought gloriously. I shall meet you blow for blow!

The land here graduated from hills to crags; the trail narrowed to a pass between two walls of sheer rock—Jat's Pass. Past the other side of this valley, the more somber hues of the Dark Circle could be glimpsed—the stunted trees, the harsh heather and gorse upon hillsides.

However, standing between them and this entryway was the strangest and most horrendous thing that Sir Godfrey Pinkham had ever seen.

It was ten feet tall. At first, Godfrey thought the hairy thing to be merely some abomination, some monster standing sentinel by the Dark Circle to repel invaders.

But when it reared to its full height and wiggled its digits and roared and peered at them through hateful bloodshot eyes, Godfrey realized that it was a gigantic severed hand.

"By Odin's eyeball," said Lord Kogar. "A little too literal a symbol for my tastes!"

Sir Mallory whooped with joy and aimed his lance. "The first obstacle in this glorious quest!" he yelled, spurring his horse toward the monster. "May God be by my side!" The thunder of hooves echoed in the valley as the knight charged the beast.

With surprising deftness, two fingers caught the lance and tossed it away. The monster hand fell upon the hapless knight, a mouth opening in its palm. It devoured Sir Mallory in a few gulps, and burped.

"I think that another tactic should be devised," said Lord Kogar's head.

chapter sixteen

Even though he had to do it almost every morning, Ian Farthing could never get used to waking up at an early hour and hauling himself from his comfortable bed. Until he woke up thoroughly perhaps a half-hour later, it felt as though he'd been drugged with some awful opiate that leached all color and hope from life, that placed him on a stinging razor edge of tears.

So when he had the opportunity—as he did this morning, presumably since his mother and father were sleeping off yesterday's excesses—he took it happily and joyfully.

Ah, he thought, lounging half-awake amid his blankets clutching his goose-down pillow like a lover, this is heaven indeed. Were I a poet, I would compose a sleepy sonnet to this state. Cruising upon Lethe, ah yes, soft and warm and floating sweetly on somnolence's raft, wafting with the soft wind of my breathing, silence the music, dream vapors the melody to this blissful rhapsody. How wonderful a hobby is sleep, simple joy in doing nothing, all memory of pain cleansed away by the susurration of my heart beating against the complete relaxation that surrounds me and . . .

Harsh, distant sounds troubled his reverie. An angry shout, the crash of wood.

Ian turned over and drew the woolen comforter around his head ever closer to shut out this disturbance. A banging at some distant door did nothing to prevent him from determinedly burrowing back into his sacred place of rest, his pleasurable cove of unconsciousness.

A hand dragged him out of sleep.

" 'Ere now, Ian," said the foggy voice of his father. "What you been up to?"

Ian sat up in bed and rubbed his eyes. Flakes of sleep dirt tumbled down onto his night-clothes.

"Up to? What do you mean, Da?"

Taking his answer from the tone of his garbled voice rather than from the words themselves, Mr. Farthing pointed a swarthy forefinger down in the general direction of the front door. "There's a bunch of townspeople down there, come to talk with you. You'd better have a word with them through our bedroom window; they don't look very happy, Ian. What's wrong, did you foul up their shoes yesterday?"

Blearily, Ian trod past the top of the steps and into his parents' room. His mother had just woken up.

"What's the commotion, then?" she demanded.

"Some village folk want to speak with Ian,"

his father said. "Don't know what about. 'Fess up, son," he said, unleashing a storm of dandruff with a scratch. "You cheat them out o' some money?"

Ian shook his head adamantly.

Mr. Farthing leaned on the sill and shouted down to the street below. "Here he be! Now what's kickin' in your pants?"

Ian inched forward furtively to get a view of this assembly. At least a dozen townsfolk were gathered in the gloomy street, holding torches and wearing unpleasant expressions. Foremost stood Hank the knacker, his face constricted with fear and outrage.

"We'd have 'im, we would, Farthing. A witch, a sorcerer is 'e, damn his eyes. The whole town see'd him yesterday behead none else but a Dark Lord, and now this mornin' the ground shakes and the sky cracks, and this evil darkness, it spills down on our innocent Mullshire."

"Aye!" said Soames Farthing, sniffing the rank air, eying the pockets of mist creeping from alley mouths. "Something does seem amiss!"

Ian shuddered. He tried to step back, but found himself paralyzed, as though the preface to an indecisive fit had seized him.

"Tell him about the dog, Hank," yelled a sallow man. "Tell him about poor Night!"

Night? thought Ian. But Night was killed by that Norx!

"This morning," said the knacker, "I hear

this scratching at my yard's gate, and I answer
. . . and it's only half my poor dog—"

Oh my God, thought Ian.

"—possessed by some evil spirit who says
that Ian Farthing is responsible for all of these
strange things happening to our beloved town.
We want him, cobbler! We want him to set
things aright, or to burn 'im. There's always
been evil hangin' around that simpleton of yours,
Soames Farthing! And now we decent folk are
payin' for your harborin' him in your home!"

"Stuff and nonsense!" said Matilda Farthing.
"They've always had it in for poor Ian. Soames!"
she ordered in a low enough voice so that those
outside could not hear. "Keep them talking.
Argue, do whatever is necessary." She grabbed
Ian by an arm and hustled him from the room.
"Come on, boy. We're going to get you out of
this house."

"Now wait a moment, Hank," said Mr. Farthing, bemusement changing to anger and determination. "You've had some wild stories in
your time, you have, but this beats all!"

Mrs. Farthing shut the door on his words,
dragging Ian behind her through the narrow
corridor to a ladder leading to the roof. "Now,
Ian, climb up on top of the roof and make your
way to the stables. It may be confounding your
problems, but steal a horse and get away from
Mullshire awhile."

Ian nodded. He'd used the ladder and the
roof many times, mostly for play. He knew
where the stables were. Still, he'd never ridden

a horse before, much less stolen one. He went
numb with the thought.

"Move, Ian. I don't want to see my son
thrown into the arms of a mob like that one."

"I love you, Mum," Ian muttered in a dead
voice as his hands reached up for the rungs.

"Shut up and get moving or I'll make you
take my cold porridge with you!" she said,
tears in her voice. "Get a move on, Ian!"

Ian climbed the ladder and pushed open the
trapdoor leading to the roof. A gust of cold air
slapped him fully awake, and he stopped with
shock.

Everything had . . . changed!

The sky, dark with fire-flecked thunderheads,
hung topsy-turvy amid an unfirm firmament.
Where the clouds broke up there were indica-
tions of stars cheek to jowl with mountains and
landscape in unholy alignment. Overhead, land
hung like the underside of some new level of
ground, the forests like clinging moss and exposed roots. Looking at this too long threat-
ened to twist Ian's sanity, and so he averted his
eyes.

The town of Mull was little better. In this
dark lighting, cloaked with shreds of clouds
and half-glimpsed differences in structure, it
looked like some evil distortion of the medieval familarity, a halfway house to Hell rather
than a simple town. The huge castle which was
its center, never famous for its warmth, looked
now as though it were carved from black ice,
sinister and stark.

The textures were all wrong, the smells misaligned, the tastes . . .

Another waft of wind buffeted Ian's clothes. The Dark Circle! It all smelled of the Dark Circle! Somehow, some of the magic had been unleashed by the cataclysm that had wrenched the sky and the land, and that magic had pooled upon Mullshire, changing it to this frightening state.

And those folk in the street thought that it was all the fault of Ian Farthing. No wonder they wanted him!

"Ian!" his mother called from below. "What's wrong?"

"Everything!" Ian whimpered.

A broomstick handle goosed him. "Get on out! At least you'll have a chance this way!"

Quite true, though Ian wondered if perhaps death itself wasn't better than venturing into this crazy-quilt new existence. Was death at all like sleep, a cozy dreamy oblivion? With his luck, it wasn't, and it seemed perfectly normal to Ian Farthing to fear death even more than this mad new configuration of heaven and earth.

He balanced his way across the roof and jumped to another, catching hold of a chimney pot. Thus, painstakingly, did he make his way across the uneven wood and tar and thatch field of the roofs toward the place he knew to be the community stables, where townspeople parked their horses.

Even from a distance, he could hear the frightened sounds of the horses, sensing something amiss in Mullshire. Perhaps, instead of taking one, he should hide in his secret place, let Hillary take care of him.

But then he remembered that Hillary was disgusted with him now, probably wanting nothing further to do with his miserable carcass. Anyway, how much longer before that mob got bigger, and started combing the nooks and crannies of Mullshire for him? No, he wouldn't be able to stay away from their clutching hands for long. His mum was right. Flight was his only recourse, and his hope lay in the stable.

There was no way through the stable roof into its interior, so Ian had to jump down into an alley. He peered through a window. Fortunately, there was no one in attendance; only horses' heads bobbed among the shadows.

He unlatched the window and clumsily slipped through, falling onto a mound of hay. He scurried up, dripping musty pieces of straw, and went toward the nearest stall. The horse penned there was a chestnut mare, with a beautiful brown mane; Ian had seen her before in the streets. Somehow he was drawn to the creature. If he was going to steal a horse, why not make it one he liked?

The horse seemed to recognize Ian as well, perhaps remembering the tidbits that he had given her from time to time. But then Ian always had had an affinity for animals; he was thankful that it had not failed him here.

Although he had never before saddled or bridled a horse, he had seen others do it and remembered the process. The steed waited patiently as Ian put the saddle on by the dim light provided from the murky outside.

Ian opened the door to the street. From the east, the direction in which his house lay, he heard voices, coming his way. He had to hurry!

His height made it difficult to mount the steed. He dragged over a small ladder and used that to aid himself. Still, in the saddle, he felt extraordinarily unsteady—as though he might slip off at any moment. All the riders he'd seen before made it look easy to travel on a horse—it wasn't!

Reflexively, he leaned forward and hugged the mare's neck, trying to direct it west away from the approaching voices and certainly away from the border of the Dark Circle.

"C'mon, my new friend," he said unsteadily in the horse's ear. "Quickly, but don't throw me off."

The horse made a strange noise. Its eyes grew wild and it bucked, almost throwing Ian off. It began to gallop east, toward the mob!

"No!" Ian cried. "Noooooooooooooo!"

He tugged hard on the reins, but to no avail; the horse seemed dead set on delivering Ian straight to his enemies. Wild visions of his fate flew through Ian's mind, and he moaned with anguish even as he held on to his unsteady purchase.

The steed ran pell-mell down the grim street, directly into the cloud of torches.

"There 'e is!" someone screamed.

"There's the bastard sorcerer!"

"Get 'im!"

"Kill the witch!"

"Burn 'im!"

These comforting words were accompanied by clutching hands, contorted features, the heat of fire, all crashing upon him like a wave.

It was madness. Ian expected to be plucked from his perch at any moment, and either be carted off to be burned at the stake or strangled on the spot. As the horse charged forward through this throng, spilling the maddened villagers, cutting through this collection of outraged and fearful humanity, Ian whimpered. Is this the end of me? he thought. Are the people who have merely tolerated me all my life finally going to have their way and snuff me out? Only the sheer might of his terror kept him clinging to his horse. Otherwise, he might have just leaped into those grabbing arms, surrendering himself as a sacrifice. . . .

A sacrifice. Would all this truly stop if he was sacrificed?

The pandemonium seemed to cease for a moment at this thought, and a brief song seemed to sing inside of Ian Farthing, and a sort of peace or tranquillity swept through him . . .

. . . and then somehow his horse broke through the crowd, picked up speed, and raced down the street away from the torches, toward the edge of the town of Mull.

"Get the horses!" someone cried.

"Don't let him get away!" screamed another.

"He mustn't make it to the Circle. God knows what might happen then!"

The Circle! Of course! The horse was galloping straight toward the border of the Dark Circle.

Or, rather, what had been the Dark Circle, before this strange and devastating change.

"No!" cried Ian Farthing into the horse's ear, tugging at the reins. The wind howled around him.

"You're going the wrong way! There's even worse danger there!"

"I'm sorry, Ian Farthing," said the horse. "But that's where you're supposed to go."

chapter seventeen

"**t**he tunes of runes in June!" whispered the stone in her ear. "Soon shall moon the loon!"

Alabaster looked up from its careful perch on the saddle, pawing its whiskers back into place after a recent jounce over a rocky patch. "So what's it got to say?" it asked.

The Norx, in if anything fouler moods than ever, bracketed Alandra's horse, regarding this new landscape with fierce suspicion and distrust.

"I shan't sing this song for long," said the rune, "but I shall play my gong."

Alandra looked down at the cat. "It's Disrupto, the rune of Confusion. The stones always give him to me while they are trying to figure something out. Apparently, they're quite baffled, and who can blame them?" Alandra shrugged. "Well, at least this little guy is entertaining."

They had been traveling now for perhaps an hour, and despite the quite spectacular morning and the new set of physical circumstances in which they found themselves, things had settled back into the usual grind.

"Put him back and pick out another. Maybe they've come up with something by now. I gave them all the information I could about Crowley Nilrem. At this point, to tell you the truth, I wish I had paid a great deal more attention to what that magician was up to."

"This game stuff is quite fascinating," said Alandra, "but frankly I find it difficult to think of myself merely as some animated piece on a gigantic board, a victim of magic manipulation." Alandra shrugged. "Oh well, from what you say, I'm a very important piece, at least."

"They Key, they say," Alabaster commented. "Although goodness knows why. You seem a normal enough prima donna—I mean, attractive and witty young lady," Alabaster put in, catching itself.

"Oh, Alabaster, I deserve so much more than this!" Alandra cried plaintively. "I am such a marvelous, special person! Beautiful! Don't you find me beautiful, Alabaster?"

"Oh, indeed so, mistress. And modest, too!"

"Yes, I've always thought so. I am such a good person, as well! My father used to tell me that. Oh, Alabaster, I miss my father so. He was the finest man who ever lived. No man shall ever again be like the man my father was! Men are such foul beasts in general, but not my father. No man shall truly have me, unless he at least tries to equal the stature of manhood my father achieved! Why, most men are no better than that ugly, twisted simpleton monster who scared Crackers so and totally fouled up my escape."

"Uhm, mistress, need I remind you that something more perhaps was occurring at that moment in the Fabric of things," Alabaster commented. "I can vouch for this, since, as you know, I had a role in the disruption."

"I find it very hard to believe all this business about games," Alandra said, "but if that is the way you care to see it, Alabaster."

"Each to his own, I suppose, mistress," said Alabaster. "Now, you mentioned trying your runes again?"

"Oh yes, I did, didn't I?"

Alandra placed Disrupto, an exaggeratedly cracked rune, back with its fellows, and then shook the pouch up for good measure.

Muffled shrieks of complaint resulted.

"Shut up, it's for your own good!" Alandra said to the runes. "What have you got to say for yourselves now?" She put her hand into the pouch and brought out one of the stones.

"So what is it?" Alabaster asked, trying to peer over her hand to get a glimpse of the stone.

Alandra was astonished.

"It's an entirely new rune!" she said. "Alabaster, this has never happened before!"

"Mistress, we're experiencing a string of such firsts, aren't we?" Alabaster meowed with faint laughter.

"I don't even know its name!"

"Why don't you ask?"

The rune consisted of three parallel lines, with two dots below them.

"Who are you?" she asked, holding this new stone up to her ear.

Orchestral music sang next to her earlobe. She shook the rune, and the sound changed to a voice speaking an indecipherable tongue.

"All right, guys, have you gone crazy with the rest of the cosmos?"

She put her hand in the bag and came back out with Orato, who was loud enough not to have to put him close to her ear. Even Alabaster could hear Orato.

"Oh truly, great and glorious queen, that would appear to be the case. In this the new rune is completely appropriate, though we confess we haven't the faintest where it came from. Popped right into our midst, it did! Calls itself Raydoee, when it calls itself anything. We haven't the faintest what it portends, but Iq— he's our smart, rational member, you know—Iq says that Raydoee picks up sounds that are soundless in the air, and gives them voice. Iq's quite a strange fellow, but he's well trained in Rune School, so we give him heed. Now what all this portends in the scheme of things, we haven't the faintest, but as you have surmised, something odd is occurring."

"Oh, thanks very much! I wouldn't have guessed!" Alandra said disgustedly. She turned to Alabaster. "Believe it or not, these guys are usually quite helpful in quotidian matters. Oh

well, I guess I'm just asking too much. A girl
can't rely on anyone these days—"

"Wait a minute," said Alabaster. "Keep that
Raydoee rune out for a moment more. It might
pick some silent sounds from the air that would
be interesting. At least it would be something
to while away the time."

Alandra shrugged. "Sure. Why not?" She held
it between them. "Here. Can you hear?"

Almost as though it had received a command,
the rune increased its volume. Strange-sounding
music poured forth awhile, then changed to
gentler tunes, then to a man speaking a language that Alandra understood.

". . . and in our Lost Pet department, we've a
polka-dotted pookah reported lost in the Eire
vicinity, Web Coordinates 46x, 56y, 84z. So all
our little greenish lepre conmen with your
crocks be on the lookout. Seamus is his name
and he plays a mean Uilean flute, so hey fairies
out there, let's get Seamus back home!

"And now, for the Hell with Health department, we have an exclusive interview with a
very important figure in the Magic Webworks,
who's afflicted with a disease that all you little
sexually active fey folk out there are going to
want to hear about. Yes, you guessed it, we
have Mr. Tom Covetit, from . . . well folks, this
is a trendy name for a world . . . The Place.
Groovy, Tommy baby."

"I can't believe I'm here."

"Just like you, Tommy. What a joker you are.
How are you feeling?"

"Grim and depressed."

"I had noticed your clenched teeth, Tommy. So, what is this awful disease you've got that makes you all the rage?"

"Herpes two."

"The sequel?"

"No, the Chronicles, stupid. Don't joke, this is serious—"

Alandra stuffed the rune back into the pouch. "I don't thing I want to hear about this disease."

"Alandra," said Alabaster. "I don't suppose you have any catnip, do you?"

"Great to get stoned, right?" said Orato. Alandra had forgotten the rune in her lap. She quickly stuffed it back in with the other runes.

"No catnip, Alabaster," Alandra said, stroking the cat with her free hand. "Perhaps we'll find some along the forest road. There seems to be a wealth of all kinds of weeds and herbs among the foliage."

"Things I've never seen before," Alabaster said. "And I should know. I'm usually on the correct level to observe."

"You're roamed through forests, Alabaster?"

"I vaguely recall something similar, though I confess most of my memories concern Crowley Nilrem's mansion."

"Think back. Perhaps there is something in your memories of those rooms—or your previous experiences—that can help us."

Alabaster closed his eyes, concentrating.

"No," he said finally. "Nothing now. Tickles on the edge of things—that's all."

"Keep on trying," Alandra said. "You never know."

The party passed on through the coiled land, through darkness and brightness, night right beside day. Alandra had grown up within the Dark Circle, and was aware of its moody, magic nature, its total unpredictability. But now with this cataclysm, everything seemed outrageously skewed. The very air held the sense of pleasure bordering on pain, excitement and possibility easily tipped into tragedy and ruin, delightful good that was evil in bright plumage.

As it happened, the first creature they encountered seemed a personification of this sense.

"Good heavens, it's a dragon," Alandra said, when the thing reared up from the side of the trail, halting their passage.

Both Toothmaw and Tombheart drew their swords.

"Please, please, let's get this right!" said the creature, standing up on two legs and spreading a wide expanse of leathery wing. "I am not a dragon. I am a *dragoon*. My father, you see, was a giant—not a terribly intelligent one, I'm afraid—and so I am by no means a full-blooded dragon."

Alandra, her startlement subsiding, could see now that the creature told the truth. Though the thing had wings and fangs and claws and such—indeed, the full complement of dragony characteristics—all these seemed touched with humanity. Its snout was short, its tail not terribly long, its claws merely second thoughts to long sensitive fingers. It wore a cap and shirt, jacket and trousers—and its eyes, though the size of playing balls, sparkled with bemused intelligence.

"I see, though, that you larger chaps are totally goonish. Well now, don't feel too bad. At least you're big."

"We are not goons," Toothmaw said. "We are of the most noble echelon of Norx, a race that once ruled an entire world. We come from a proud and noble heritage, and do not take well to slander, no matter who it is from."

"Hmm. Touchy fellows, eh? Well, I shall be short and let you be on your way. I was just on a little refreshing jaunt—my home is on top of one of those mountains yonder, you see—and then things just went topsy-turvy. Positively Wagnerian. The ruckus was so great, I dropped like a stone from the sky and woke up here just a little while ago, simply astonished at what has come to pass. I don't suppose any of you folks can give me a clue, could you? It's very upsetting, and I'm sure that the citizens of my humble retreat would very much like to know just what has tossed our modest magical existence into such a"—he looked about him, groping for the proper term—"madhouse."

Alandra had an idea.

She smiled as sweetly as she could, and she batted her beautiful blue eyes at the dragoon and spoke in a voice that was amazingly close to a coo. "Good, kind, dragoon! You are such a handsome beast. Don't you think so, Alabaster?"

"Oh yes, mistress, a fine handsome fellow if ever I saw one!"

"I'll bet, Alabaster, that this splendid prince among dragoons is waited on hand and foot by the most beautiful of virgins."

The dragoon primped a bit, taking pleasure in the compliment. "Well, madam, actually no. I'm a bachelor, and while I've a goodly assortment of company back at my hold, there are no beautiful virgins."

"No virgins!" said Alandra. "What kind of life do you have, unblessed by the occasional virgin kiss upon your handsome countenance?"

"Not so bad, actually, though the notion sounds pleasant!"

"Away, beast!" cried Tombheart. "We must continue our journey!" The Norx glanced askance at Alandra. "You are a strange one, oh queen. Consorting with such beasts."

"No, truly, I find this most diverting," she said brightly. "You don't want to bring home an unhappy queen to her dear husband, do you? Why, I can tell him that we met this delightful dragoon and had a delightful chat. Now tell me, dragoon—"

"Princerik, madam," the dragoon interrupted cordially.

"Yes, Princerik. A lovely name. You are such a cutie pie, and I hate to think that you have spent your days without the brush of a virgin's lips over your green cheeks. As it happens, I am a virgin and intend to right this freak of nature by making you a satisfied and complete dragoon!"

"Oh queen," said Toothmaw, wielding his sword. "Do not—"

Tombheart held up a restraining hand. "We cannot allow this, oh queen. To come too close to such a beast is dreadfully dangerous." He tightened the slack on the leather leash, reminding Alandra who was in control."

"A virgin?" the dragoon said excitedly, eyes rolling, a suggestion of smoke wisping up from its wide-veined nostrils. "And you so beautiful! Beauty and virginity are a rare combination, and I confess, the notion of being kissed by such a damosel awakes deep longings in this beastly breast. Gentle Norx, would you permit the lady—"

"Step not one yard closer, brute!" Tombheart growled in warning. "We are sworn to our lady's protection!"

"Oh, pshaw and pshakespeare!" Alandra said. "Oh, how frustrated I am. A handsome dragoon to kiss before me, and I am prevented from fulfilling a destiny I have always desired." She sighed, making sure her breast heaved provocatively. "Oh, how many times have I dreamed that a charming dragoon would carry me away to his lair and shower me with ancient treasure. But alas, this is too much to ask of this warped reality, that passionate dreams come true!"

"Mistress, what are you doing?" Alabaster asked tremulously, his hackles rising.

The dragoon's wings were trembling. Spastic tics began to move over its face. "And such a lovely piece of femininity!" it said, its previously benign aspect changing to bestial lust. "Ah, such delicious limbs, such a savory scent!" Drool dripped from its mouth as the eyes bugged, hungrily examining the bare leg that Alandra had teasingly exposed.

"Queen," said Toothmaw, "we must travel. Cease this disgraceful exhibition."

But Alandra's flirtations had clearly had effects upon Princerik. The creature quivered and snorted, shaking with excitement. "I must have it," he said. "I must have my kiss. I must have a thousand kisses!"

Alandra mimed a juicy kiss at the dragoon as the Norx hustled her away, causing a jet of steam to stream from the creature's mouth.

It happened so quickly that even Alandra was surprised, though it was what she had played for. The dragoon hopped onto the trail and raced up to Alandra. With one set of claws, it cut off the leather leash, and with the other it knocked Tombheart to the ground. Then it plucked Alandra off her horse and gathered her to its chest with a strange combination of passion and tenderness.

Alabaster clung for dear life.

Toothmaw swung his horse about to do battle, but the bulky Norx was much too slow; the dragoon leaped into the air, unfurled its wings, and began to flap them mightily.

Up and up they flew, Alabaster shrieking

with fear, Alandra herself feeling a touch of dizzy vertigo. Behind they left the maddened Norx, waving their useless swords wildly, bellowing obscenities that were soon swallowed up by the thunder of powerful wings smiting the air.

"Oh, I can't thank you enough!" Alandra said finally, joyfully, to the dragoon. "Those dreadful smelly things had me captive and were taking me exactly where I didn't want to go! You seemed such a brave, civilized dragoon. I knew you would save me. Now, if you would be so kind, could you carry my dear Alabaster and me to the border where my predicted handsome knight rescuer Sir Godfrey awaits? And I shall give you the most wonderful virgin kiss your proud and noble heart could ever hope for!"

"My sweet and succulent morsel!" the dragoon said. A drop of rancid spittle leaked onto Alandra's head. "Now that I hold you in my arms, how can I ever let you go? I shall take you to my mountain demesne and there you shall kiss me and kiss me again, and we shall live happily ever after. Oh, wait until Alison sees you. Oh calloo callay, I am a lonely dragoon no more!"

"Oh, dear," said Alandra. "I fear, Alabaster, that I have made a slight miscalculation!"

Alabaster let a sob suffice as answer.

chapter eighteen

lthough during the course of the breakneck rush across the fields and plains of Mull-shire Ian Farthing constantly attempted communication with the spirit possessing the chestnut steed, the beast never spoke to him again.

As the familiar scenery flew past, and the howling and chill wind whipped Ian, he considered jumping off. However two considerations gave him pause.

For one thing, the horse was going incredibly fast—faster than Ian had ever seen a horse go before. Of course, he'd never been atop one running before, so perhaps it was this unique vantage point that made the difference. Still, the notion of jumping off right now seemed foolhardy. With Ian Farthing's luck, he'd break his neck.

And even if he wasn't harmed, there was the second consideration to heed: There was a maddened mob after him. On foot, he didn't have much of a chance to hide from them, much less escape this area.

No, the only hope was to hang on to the mare and let it take him wherever it was going.

There was hardly time, in his terror, for Ian Farthing to give much thought to his peculiar set of circumstances, but he was able to think about what the horse had said to him.

Where he was *supposed* to go? The statement reeked of predestination, which Ian found peculiar and unlikely—not that such a concept could not be true, only that he should somehow be an important figure in the scheme of things.

But then, the way—the perverse way—that things were happening, no doubt another mistake had been made. Which, all in all, would not surprise him much at all.

Ian had the fanciful notion that when he stood before God Himself at Judgment Day, he'd make it into the lower levels of Heaven by simple obscurity. He wasn't important enough to be given a thorough going-over from the Book of Life, or to be scrutinized by God Himself. No, some mousy little clerk in a musty room would read his life, then figure out the cost of sending this insignificant cypher to Hell—and decide that it would be too expensive. If Ian Farthing escaped simple Oblivion and made it to the shores of Heaven, it would merely be because heavenly folks needed the odd shoe repaired.

There was nothing sensible to do. He could

only cling to the top of the horse, wherever it was going, and hope for the best. Sometimes Ian found that it was best to just let himself go in the direction Fate seemed to be taking him, to not merely resign himself to that course, but to choose it.

Alas, bumping up and down on this mad willy-nilly dash toward what surely must be perdition, Ian Farthing could only feel resigned.

If Mullshire had become like this, goodness knew what the border was like! What dread monsters had been unearthed? Look at what had happened the last time he had ventured near that place!

How long he bounced and jounced upon that mad spirit-possessed horse he never knew; there was only the smell of horse sweat, the taste of fear in his mouth, and the swirling contrasts of color and darkness moiling before him for what seemed like an eternity.

Suddenly, Ian was aware of passing between rocks. The horse stopped so suddenly, only his frenzied grip on the saddle kept him from being tossed off ass over ankles.

Then he was aware of voices. Shouts? Definitely there were people about. But in his dizzy state, he could not tell exactly who. He felt as though the whole universe were swirling about him, quite insanely.

"Well now," a voice said. "Look who's here!"

"Ermmmmhhhhh," said Ian Farthing.

"Let's help him off the horse, now, shall we? Clearly he's come to give us the benefit of his might and bravery, but he looks a bit worse for the ride. In a hurry are you, Ian Farthing? So eager are you to show us your true talents?"

Ian tried to see who was speaking to him, but everything was blurry.

Strong hands helped him down from the mare, set him on his feet.

"Right, Ian Farthing. You are a brave and noble lad, and we are truly and heartily sorry for ever doubting you."

A pat on the back almost sent him face first into the ground.

"Give him that strange sword," said another voice. "That might help. It seems to work for him."

Sword? Why would he need a sword?

"An excellent idea. Ronald, dear boy. I believe it's in your pack. There's a good lad. Here, Ian."

A cylinder was thrust into his hand. Ian had recovered sufficiently to see that it was the item that he had found in the midst of the fair, the thing that Kogar had called the Pen That Is Mightier Than the Sword, just before it had cut off the fellow's head.

Then he felt two sets of hands to either side of him grab his arms and hustle him along.

"What are you doing?" Ian demanded, still too dazed to give any actual physical objection to this treatment. He twisted his head to one side. His vision had cleared sufficiently to make out one of the men who was hurrying him wherever.

Godfrey Pinkham!

"Godfrey!" he said, "what are you doing?"

"Happy to see me then, are you, Ian Farthing? Now, all we ask, dear chap, is for you to show a little bit of the spunk that we saw just yesterday. And if you don't have it . . . well, we haven't lost much, have we lads?"

From behind arose voices in agreement.

It was the rescue party for Princess Alandra. But what did they need him for?

With little ceremony, the two knights heaved Ian into a narrow stretch of trail. He stumbled and fell down. He began to cough.

"Get up then, Ian Farthing, or you'll wish you had," called a voice from behind. "And we'll not abide any more show of cowardice, simpleton. Sir Mortimer here has a very accurate crossbow that he'll be happy to use should you turn coward again. Give us a good fight, then, Ian! Let's see what you are really made of!"

Ian saw that, indeed, one of the knights held a crossbow.

But why had they thrown him in this alley-like construction of a trail?

His answer came first as a hoarse, loud roar.

Ian almost jumped out of his boots at the sound. Startled, he swung around and found himself facing what the knights wanted him to fight.

The thing was ten yards away. It did not advance, although it seemed to want to. It was as though the thing was some kind of guardian, expressly put there to prevent entrance into the Dark Circle.

The fingers were thick and bulbous, purpled with throbbing veins. Its hair was matted with blood, only part of which came from the quarrels that the knights had tried to kill it with. Its eyes, set deep into two of the fingertips, were cruel and milky, and an intelligence burned within them.

The intelligence recognized Ian Farthing.

And then Ian Farthing realized what the thing was.

"Oh my sweet living God!" he said.

It was a gigantic hairy hand—the hand that he had cut from the Norx in the quagmire!

How could it still be alive?

How could it have grown so?

"Ian Farthing!" it said, using a truly obscene mouth in its swarthy palm. "Come! I hunger!"

Ian turned, fear propelling his action. His immediate instinct, as usual, was to run.

But his eyes immediately aligned upon the crossbow aimed directly at him.

"No, no, Ian," said Sir Godfrey. "You don't seem to understand. You are there to do battle, not to turn tail."

Ian looked down at the pen. He touched the stud, and the amazingly sharp rapier blade grew out of one end. It glistened, as though from its own interior light.

"But Godfrey!" Ian said. "Going against that thing is suicide!"

"No free ride for you, Ian Farthing. If you

want to come with us, you're going to have to rid the path of that monster."

Speaking did no good—they couldn't even understand him!

Ian tried to swallow and realized he could not. His mouth was dry with fear. He turned to face the beast, and he thought: Whatever I do, I'm going to die. Perhaps I can die bravely, instead of like a coward. Hillary was right. Even if there was nothing essentially brave inside him, there was enough emptiness within to fill with some kind of substitute.

Tentatively, he stepped forward, holding the sword out in his crooked grasp.

The hand growled, its fingers wiggling grotesquely, like a sea urchin's tentacles in a current.

Ian jumped back, trembling.

This was total foolishness. Never in a million years could a bent dwarvish simpleton take on such a monster, even with the clearly special sword he held.

"Godfrey! Please! Don't make me fight this thing!" he screamed, tears stinging his eyes. "There must be some other way of dealing with it!"

"What did you say, Ian Farthing?" responded Sir Godfrey Pinkham. "I can't understand you. Now get on with it! Either you'll kill the thing with sword or poison it with your foul carcass!"

Pure rage cleansed Ian of fear for the moment. He'd show that arrogant bastard!

With a scream, he charged the creature, limping frantically, sword outstretched.

One of the fingers dodged the blade and neatly smacked Ian on the side, hurtling him against rock. He bounced off and rolled away, somehow managing to keep hold of his sword without hurting himself.

Groaning, he picked himself up, flinching at the thought of the hand about to slap him down.

But it did not move; apparently it was content to stay in its defensive position, at an angle where it was safe from the knight's crossbow.

"*That was stupid, Ian Farthing,*" said a strangely familiar voice.

Ian twirled around. "Who said that?"

"*I did, you lamebrain.*"

The voice seemed to come from within him, just as it had the last time he had dealt with the Norx.

"Who are you?" he asked desperately.

"*That's for you to discover on your own, my friend,*" said the inner voice. "*For now, I suggest you take my suggestion and forget about trying to deal with this hand monster at close quarters. You just don't have the leverage right now. You'll have the chance to maybe carve off a finger before the beast swallows you whole.*"

"So wonderful. So what do I do?" Ian screamed.

"So now he's talking to himself!" Godfrey cried. "So have at the beast, Ian! Alandra's getting farther away at every moment! Slice it up or we'll bury a quarrel in that yellow spine of yours."

"The magic of the pen is stronger here, close to the Circle. Perhaps there are other ways to use it. Give it a go."

Ian touched the stud on the pen again, and the rapier blade withdrew.

"Okay. What now?"

"I don't know," said the inner voice. *"I'm not all-seeing. Try writing with it."*

"Oh, sure, we'll kill it by drawing a mustache on it!"

"No, don't write on it. Write on yourself."

"Write what?"

"I don't know. Write 'magical hand' on your palm."

"You must be joking."

"Look, I didn't steer you wrong last time, did I? Give it a try."

Ian took the pen and wrote the words on his left palm.

"Okay, now, point your forefinger at the hand and direct a magical blast at the beast!" directed the inner voice.

Ian obeyed, pointing his hand right above the mouth.

"Fire!" he commanded.

"But nothing happened.

"Look, I'm not perfect," said the inner voice. *"But there really must be something special about that pen."*

"I don't seem to have time to find out!" Ian

said, feeling close to panic. "I'm caught between two rocks and two hard places!"

There was no response. The inner voice was gone. What was he doing, talking to himself, anyway? A sure first sign of encroaching insanity.

Sane or insane, it looked as though he was about to die.

That thought somehow cleared his head.

If he was going to die, he might as well get it over with.

He pressed the tab on the pen again, and the rapier returned.

"Very well, hand," Ian Farthing said, stepping forward. "Let's see—"

The hand opened its mouth and roared.

Ian tripped. The rapier flew from his hand, flying point first straight into the creature's mouth.

The giant hand gurgled with pain. It staggered backward, its digits wiggling madly.

"Quickly!" Ian yelled. "Bring on your crossbow! Give me another sword! I've hurt the thing!"

"Good God!" said Godfrey Pinkham. "I can understand the bastard! Here, lads, do as he says. Have we got a spare sword?" A weapon was thrust into his hands. He ran forward and handed it to Ian. "Good show there, Ian. I always knew you had it in you!"

Ian found himself smiling as two crossbowmen shouldered past him in pursuit of the gigantic hand. He took the proffered sword and advanced into the coming fray.

Somehow, the ordeal had not left him breathless. For some reason, he felt stronger!

With a *thwip!* another quarrel buried itself in
the hairy flesh of the hand. The next brought a
howl of pain. It had backed into a clearing, and
was now weaving back and forth.

Riding the thrill of the moment, Ian brought
up his sword and was about to charge when
the monster's voice stopped him. "Halt, Ian
Farthing!" it said, gargling its own blood. "Strike
no more blows. You have killed me already,
and I would speak with you."

"Very well," said Ian, keeping his sword up
nonetheless. "What do you have to say?"

"The hounds of Hell are loosed, the Doom
Games knell like bells without clappers. All
ends unravel into simple means. Take heed
those who would truly quest, for death is the
only true destiny. The powers that are loosed
today are darker than you know."

The hand keeled over, gasped, and died.

"Pleasant message!" said Godfrey. "Well,
you've done a good job, Ian Farthing. And my
goodness . . . you've changed somewhat. How
curious!"

Changed? thought Ian. Whatever did Godfrey
mean?

A commotion among the other knights di-
verted his attention. "There's a bunch of horsemen coming from Mull, Godfrey! And they're
in a hurry!"

"They're after me," Ian said.

"Damn, I can't understand you again. For

a moment I could," said Godfrey, clearly baffled but elated at the clearing of the monstrous obstruction in their path. "Why do you suppose these Mullshire folk have journeyed all the way out here in these strange climes?"

"Perhaps I should be moving along," suggested Ian, starting to walk away.

"Here, here," said Godfrey, catching him up in his powerful grasp. "Stick around. I must try to figure out how to speak with you, Ian Farthing. You might not be as simple as I've thought. In fact, you could be of great use to our expedition."

"But those people want to kill me!" Ian cried, his excitement mauling his words even further from recognition. He tried to break free from the knight's hold but found that his former strength and feelings of well-being had deserted him entirely.

"Here, here, Ian!" Godfrey said. "I know you're in a hurry to help save Alandra, but we can wait a few minutes to see what these villagers want."

With angry cries and horse sounds, the villagers swooped into the valley. Ian cringed away from their entry.

"What can I do for you, goodly Mullshire folk?" Sir Godfrey addressed the new arrivals in a loud voice ringing with authority.

At the forefront of the mob was Hank the knacker, much the worse for his mad ride. He'd also managed to singe some of his hair in his torch, which he'd had the wisdom to discard before he mounted his horse.

"There he is! There's the evil sorcerer who has brought this doom down around our heads!" cried the knacker. "Give him to us, so we can burn him!"

Godfrey blinked. "Evil sorcerer? Who, this goodly fellow here? Why, surely you must jest."

The waving pitchforks and smoking torches and growling demands underlined the villagers' intentions.

"Apparently not," said Sir Godfrey. "Well, I assure you, there must be some mistake. I'll grant you there's something odd about this chap, but I really don't think we can blame him for all that's happened!"

"My dead dog told me so!" Hank the knacker proclaimed.

"Well, that may be, but did your dead dog tell you that by burning Ian Farthing, everything would be put aright?" Godfrey demanded.

"Well, er, no, not actually, but it stands to reason—"

"I see no reason upon your countenances, Mullshire folk. You only seek a scapegoat upon whom to vent your rage and uncertainty. Believe me, killing Ian Farthing will do absolutely nothing to right the way that things have become. Only the mission of us knights can possibly help. . . . And this goodly lad has aided us already by helping to defeat a creature blocking our pathway. Is this the work of an evil sorcerer, people? I say nay! And I request that you belay your foolish desire for the fellow's blood and leave him in our charge!"

One of the horsemen dismounted. Ian recognized him as the old farmer whose shoe he had fixed the day before. A look of astonishment was plain on his face as he shoved aside Hank the knacker and walked toward Ian.

"Saints alive! I thought you looked familiar, Ian Farthing," said the man. "And now, your face has altered somewhat, and you look even more like him. . . ."

"Like who, sirrah?" Godfrey demanded, extending his sword as warning and in possible defense.

"Like the boy who fell from the rent in the sky. My vision I seen, years and years ago. He weren't no twisted dwarf, that little boy, but he had those eyes, and some of that face," said Jacob Tillster.

"You see?" cried the knacker. "He is sent as a curse from Perdition."

"Weren't no Perdition I seen in that boy that dropped on my field! He was like an angel, he was. Cherubic, in fact! Beautiful."

"What happened then?" Godfrey asked, bemused.

"Why, then I don't know. I fainted dead away, I did. Woke up with a terrible headache, half blinded by all that light, and only remembered the full vision years later!" He wagged his finger at Ian. "God help me, you look different now, older and uglier, but you're the one I saw, Ian Farthing."

"Me?" Ian said disbelievingly. "Fall from the sky? That's rubbish!"

The peasant farmer fell to his knees before Ian. "Might I kiss your hand?"

Before he could remonstrate, Ian found his hand being slobbered over.

"Thank you," said the old peasant. "With your blessing I can die complete."

Another horse bounded into the assembly, bearing Hillary Muffin. She jumped off the horse and ran over to Ian. "Oh Ian, Ian, are you all right? Ian, what has happened?"

Godfrey made a move to push the new arrival away, but Ian gestured that she was no threat.

"I know as much as you do, Hillary. I only know that these people think it was my fault, and I had to get away."

"Ian! You look different! What has happened?" Hillary said.

"I don't know. I just . . . er . . . helped Godfrey and these knights through a sticky situation, and by doing so . . . I changed!"

"I told you, Ian. I told you there was something special about you, Ian Farthing!" Hillary cried joyfully. "I knew it. All my life I knew it!"

"Pardon me, young lady," said Godfrey. "but apparently you understand this fellow! Would you be so kind as to translate what he has to say to these townspeople so that they can go back to their homes and let us be about our knightly quest?"

"Certainly," responded Hillary. "Ian, what have you got to say?"

"I can say that I don't want to be here, Hillary. Godfrey has got it into his noggin that I should come along on this crazy quest, and frankly I'm scared out of my mind at the notion!"

"Ian, don't you see?" Hillary said enthusiastically. "That's perfectly normal. Everyone is scared. And can't you also see that this is what you're supposed to do? You have the opportunity now to find out who you really are! You're changing already, I can see!"

"He's an angel," the peasant repeated. "Young girl, he's the angel I seen fall from the sky!"

Ian shook his head emphatically. "I'm no angel. I'm just a simpleton, and I wish people would leave me be. All I want to do is cobble shoes, Hillary. That's all I ask from life."

"Now that's not true, Ian Farthing. You've told me your dreams, and they certainly don't include cobbling. So are you going to speak to these village folk? They need some reassurance, Ian. And from the looks of it, you're the only one who can do it. If not for yourself, then do it for them, do it for the faith that I've had in you all my life!"

Ian Farthing bit his lip. Could this truly be? Could it be possible that he wasn't just a twisted simpleton, doomed to a life of jeers and squalor? That's what that nagging inner voice had said, and that's what everything in these past days had pointed to.

A feeling of emptiness opened in him. He had never felt so frightened in his life.

He wasn't who he thought he was! There was something much deeper, much more important to him, and the notion made him feel more lost and alone than he ever had before.

Then he looked out at the faces of the village people, and he saw, no, felt that same fear and sense of dislocation in their faces. It truly wasn't his death that they wanted ... it was hope, reassurance, a sense of rearranged balance.

All eyes were on him, and despite himself, he found himself speaking to them.

"I guess I'm like everyone," he began haltingly, and Hillary interpreted what he said, though somehow, most of Ian's words were clearer now, better pronounced. "I've found myself in a situation that was not of my own making, yet made the best of it. Played my part, just asking for what any human wants—work, play, a little love, the hope of fulfillment. Now I find that I have a chance for more than that. Fellow villagers, please believe me, I did not cause this Bedlam Day, and I do not deserve to die for it. I have no idea of the meaning of this ... the meaning of anything, anymore. Meaning has no meaning in this new world, and I have to search for that meaning. So please, let me be with my curse. And if somehow my actions and discoveries in this quest into the Dark Circle prove to right the course of things, then that is all the meaning I can ever ask for."

Heads nodded thoughtfully. The looks on the

faces of the villagers changed, and there were murmurs of "God be with thee" and "Good luck, you'll need it!" They got back onto their horses and quietly dispersed back to whatever they could reassemble of their own lives.

Hillary hugged Ian's arm. "Oh, that was wonderful, Ian! They listened to you. They can see that really you are just as good as they are. Better!"

"Just as scared," said Ian. "Just as confused."

"What did he say?" asked Godfrey.

"He says that he's all ready to go, Sir Godfrey, but of course he's going to need me to come along and speak for him!"

"Hillary, no! That's too dangerous!" said Ian. "If anything happened to you—"

"Why, that can certainly be arranged," said Sir Godfrey, a gleam entering his eye. "We should be glad of feminine company. We can practice our chivalry even as we go aquesting!"

"You see Ian, you are outvoted."

Ian started to object, then let it go. The truth was that if he was bound for some obscure destiny, then he was glad of company as good as Hillary's. He decided to allow himself that selfishness.

"We shall have to recover my pen inside that swollen Norx hand," Ian told Sir Godfrey through Hillary. "And there's another sword that I've hidden quite nearby that we should retrieve. I think it might be of some use."

"Whatever you say, Master Ian Farthing," said Sir Godfrey, placing a hand upon Ian's shoulder.

"And may I take this opportunity to welcome you to our august company. We have quite a journey in store for us all, a beautiful princess to save, and something absolutely divine about the whole quest. I knew that one day being a knight would truly amount to something."

Ian turned to look out over the topsy-turvy horizon. What magic, what evil, what misadventures lurked in all that confusion, waiting for him?

He still wasn't sure if he really wanted to know.

epilog

Crowley Nilrem the magus rooted through the steamer trunk filled with ancient packs of Tarot cards, nose cringing at the smell of mothballs that wafted from the large piles. There were all kinds of decks, of course, from Abyssinian to Zoroastrian; a few even had pictures of nude women on their backs. They would all do. After all, it wasn't the deck, it was the dealer. But Crowley Nilrem had several favorites, cards that he felt most comfortable with, and so it was these he looked for to utilize on his journey.

Plaster spilled onto his head from the cracked ceiling. He barely noticed by now; it had become a regular occurrence. His mansion was falling to pieces, and he had to travel immediately to his closest Gaming Magus neighbor. There he could achieve the proper foundation for the summoning of the Nine for a council.

Councils were dreadful, nasty affairs, since the Gaming Magi generally despised one another, but under these circumstances nothing else was suitable to deal with this frightening matter at hand.

"Ah!" said Crowley Nilrem, finding the packs he was looking for. Hastily, he stuffed the principal pack—Egyptian, particularly good for playing pinochle—and two sets of spares into the voluminous pockets of his tweed coat, already packed with other oddments he might need for spells once he ventured outside his sphere of Direct Influence.

The house rumbled and shuddered.

He must hurry. No waiting could be tolerated; he must reach the periphery as soon as possible so that he could put the Stasis Enchantment into effect.

He ran out of the library without even stopping to check the gaming room to see if there was any change in the configuration of the Gaming Board. The sight of that thing would only depress him even more, and he needed every facet of his magical powers, every bit of his concentration, to complete the speedy Transit that his specially treated cards could effect.

Tails aflap behind him, he dashed through the front double doors of the mansion, not even bothering to close them. Outside, the weather was a murky mess of strangely lit fog, swirling and flowing in odd moisture dances. He traipsed through the wet grasses, careful of his footing. Goodness knew, with things as they were, potholes might have opened; nothing could be so hazardous at this time.

Fortunately, if any had opened, he avoided

them, making his way through his lovely garden, through a copse of trees and from there to the edge. Here, as though it met some kind of invisible wall, the fog stopped. Crowley Nilrem stepped into clear starlight.

The edge of his property was ragged, complete with roots straggling out from the ground like filthy frozen snakes. Nilrem favored this uprooted effect, though he could have changed it. Whether or not this island in the Ocean of Night and its old gabled manse had actually ever been anywhere else, the magus did not know. He had inherited it from Gaming Magus Chauncey Fothergay, after that worthy had been persuaded to retire, and its history was not readily available.

From this viewpoint, the cosmos appeared peaceful enough this day. The nebulae and galaxies shone splendidly. The occasional comet or meteor hurtled by, apparently unperturbed. Neighboring planets had not changed colors.

Still, appearances were not only decieving, Nilrem knew, sometimes they were a total sham.

He wasted no time star-gazing. He picked out a vial from his pocket, poured some of the previously prepared compound into his hand, and tossed it into the fog, shouting the appropriate spell.

Immediately the roiling fog stopped. The specks of tossed magical matter hung in the air like magnified snowflakes. Sudden branches of energy connected them, creating a domed webwork completely around the island.

Satisfied, Nilrem turned to his next task.

He drew a set of Tarot cards bearing pictures of pyramids on their backs and shuffled them without turning them over. The journey could be long or short—it depended upon when one of the destination cards appeared in the spread.

Nilrem intoned the correct words, then took the topmost card and turned it over. Eight of cups. How appropriate; the card signifying a search for new paths. Nilrem threw the card into space. It stopped just two feet away from the precipice, one foot above the ground level, suspended.

Crowley Nilrem stepped upon it as though it were a stair. Immediately, the surroundings shifted from his island in stasis, to a land of blizzard. Shivering, Nilrem drew and threw the next card, taking no time to note its significance; that could be read later, when the cards reformed at the bottom of the deck. From wind and snow, to a desert world; from sands and sun, to a cloudy clime; from wet and rain, to a rainbow world: the magus stepped from reality to reality as though they were steps in a stairwell.

Finally, he drew the correct card, the High Priest.

His mother had suggested that the most spiritual member of the Nine, Jason Dunworthy, might have the necessary answers. Besides, whenever the Nine had to call a conference, that event occurred in Dunworthy's estate, since it had the calmest atmosphere.

Nilrem stepped upon the card, and the scene shifted away from a flowery garden to a hedged field in front of a country manor. Unseen birds trilled pleasantly in nearby woods. There was the scent of mown grass, the taste of spring. Chill nipped the air.

Nilrem picked up the High Priest and summoned back the other cards. He brushed himself off as best he could, hoping that Dunworthy would excuse his appearance, considering the circumstances.

The front door had a dragon's-head knocker. Nilrem knocked. No one answered. The magus tried the knob; the door was open, so he stepped into the foyer.

The Dunworthy domicile was radically different from Crowley Nilrem's estate. For one thing, its spacious interior was quite orderly. The rooms had an Art Nouveau feel; curlicued columns, stuffed peacocks, and swirling drapes all contributed to this effect, to say nothing of the elaborate Persian rugs. Everything was elegant and spotlessly clean, cloaked in a trace of lemon-wax scent.

"Hullo?" Crowley Nilrem said. "Anyone here?"

Curious. No servants about, either.

"Dunworthy? Hullo, old chap? Are you home?" Nilrem began exploring the rooms.

Nothing seemed amiss; everything was in its place, from divans to doorstops.

Jason Dunworthy's Gaming Room, Nilrem remembered, was in the west wing. The magus set out to locate it, thinking that surely, what with recent events, that was where Dunworthy would be.

Along the hallway paraded portraits of ancestors and previous occupants of this manor, dressed in a bewildering array of costumes and hats, but all wearing similar expressions of bemused arrogance common to the Gaming Magi.

Why, thought Crowley Nilrem, did I have to choose this profession?

It had been so much fun at first, this work that was play, this play that was work. Play, after all, was the very foundation of creation; games were logical extensions of this principle. That the structure of the multiverse should eventually depend upon Gaming Magic was inevitable. What higher aspiration for a thinking being than to become a magician of the dice, the source of the enchanted clickings of chance in the gaming rooms of existence?

However, absorbing as it had become, the role of Gaming Magus was a tiger by the tail, and Crowley Nilrem was feeling its teeth.

Ah! There was the entrance, just ahead.

A sign above the door read:

ABANDON CASH ALL YE WHO ENTER HERE.

Dunworthy always had been a bit of a joker, not an unusual trait for Gaming Magi who had stayed around for a while. Hence, some of the more absurd and amusing appendix capsules, where strategy and tactics were tested before being employed in the general cosmos. In fact, Dunworthy was something of a specialist in creating these simulacrum worlds expressly for the amusement and instruction of himself and his fellows. Even now, his Gambler's World was still a weekend's respite for all manner of magicians in the know, and a steady source of revenue for Jason Dunworthy.

Nilrem knocked on the door.

"Dunworthy? You there, old boy? Bit of a snit we're in, wot? It's Crowley, Jason. Be a good fellow and let me in."

Nilrem's words were greeted with silence.

The magus waited a moment, then tried the door.

It was open. Nilrem entered.

Jason Dunworthy's Gaming Room looked much like his colleague's, save that like the rest of his establishment, it was much neater, more compartmentalized.

And, as in Nilrem's room, currently his central Gaming Board depicting the Dark Circle had changed configuration. It hung just below the ceiling, in the shape of a ragged Moebius strip.

Hanging from the Gaming Board by a rope tied to one foot was Jason Dunworthy.

His long silvery hair, speckled with blood, hung down, barely touching the top of his elaborately carved Gaming Table. His hands were tied behind his back.

His position resembled that of the Tarot's Hanged Man.

"Dunworthy!" cried Crowley Nilrem.

He went to his colleague and occasional

opponent. Was there a knife about anywhere? He had to cut the poor chap down.

Dunworthy's eyes opened.

"Ow!" he said.

"Dunworthy! What happened, old man?"

Dunworthy's bleary eyes searched out the owner's voice. "Haven't . . . long . . ." he said.

He twisted a little, and Nilrem gasped.

Embedded in one of the man's temples was a large spiked four-sided die. A dribble of blood leaked out with the movement, splattering on the table.

"He's back," said Dunworthy. "I tried to stop him with the crystal. . . . Take it."

"Yes, old man, I know he's back, but right now we'll have to get you down and set up some kind of healing spell."

"No . . . listen! Seven fours in a row on the crystal die! Seven fours in a row on the Die of Dances and—"

Jason Dunworthy shuddered and died.

Nor could he be recalled by magical means, for he had been killed by a magical item, the Die of Dances.

With great sadness, Crowley Nilrem found a knife and cut his colleague down. He pried the die from its place in the dead magus's head and cleaned it off with a rag.

The Die of Dances was one of the Original Set, the Destiny Dice. From these dice had been sculpted the Gaming Magic that controlled the multiverse. Each of the Gaming Magi owned at least one, capable of various powers. Nilrem's pair, the Eyes of Ivory, lay snug and safe in his pocket by the packs of cards. The Die of Dances, though, was of the Primary Set that had manufactured the Goal Rolls—this pyramid-shaped bit of unknown substance had often lain in the Creator's hand ... and that dreaded Other's hand as well. It was known as the Die of Dances because of its tendency to bounce and spin on its ends like a dancing top before it finally settled on one end. Unlike the other dice, the significant number was the numeral undisplayed. Thus, this was a die of the undercurrents of events, the hidden and the paradoxical.

He set it aside, then drew his Tarot card pack.

All of the cards he had used, including the High Priest, had changed to the Hanged Man.

Nilrem gritted his teeth, then carefully picked out the remaining seven Gaming Magi members and formed a pentacle on the Gaming Table, using the cards as symbolic intersection points of imaginary lines. He placed his own card in the center. This would call the others for a council.

Crowley Nilrem took off his coat and rolled up his sleeve.

He looked sadly at the body of Jason Dunworthy, covered now by a sheet. He was changing the rules indeed, the bastard. One of the prime rules had been that Gaming Magi were simply not harmed.

Crowley Nilrem sat down at the Gaming Table, combing back his mop of hair with his fingers.

So. It had come to this, he thought sadly. After all of his effort, all of his gaming, it had come back to the Die of Dances, a die that had always caused woe, a die barely constrained by the statistical laws of chance, a die the magi thought might have some obscure alien life of its own.

Wondering what would happen this time, Crowley Nilrem picked up the crystalline die, still stained with Gaming Magi blood despite the cleaning, and began to roll.

about the author

DAVID BISCHOFF was born December 15, 1951, in Washington, D.C., and grew up in the D.C. suburbs carousing with Air Force brats near Andrews Air Force Base. He graduated from the University of Maryland in 1973 with a B.A. in TV and Film and worked for six years with NBC Washington, then became a full-time freelance writer.

He has written a number of novels, including *Nightworld*, *Star Fall*, *Mandala*, *Day of the Dragonstar* (with Thomas F. Monteleone), *The Selkie* (with Charles Sheffield), available in a Signet edition, and the upcoming *Infinite Battle* and *The Crunch Bunch*, not to mention the next two volumes of *The Books of the Gaming Magi*.

His short work has appeared in such magazines as *Omni*, *Analog*, *The Magazine of Fantasy and SF*, and *Amazing*, as well as a number of original anthologies.

He has served as both secretary and vice-president of the Science Fiction Writers of America.

Bischoff loves movies, rock and British folk, and other things too humorous to mention. He now lives in Silver Spring, Maryland.

JOIN THE *GAMING MAGI* READERS' PANEL

Help us bring you more of the books you like by filling out this survey and mailing it in today.

1. Book Title: _____
   Book #: _____

2. Using the scale below, how would you rate this book on the following features?

POOR		NOT SO GOOD			O.K.		GOOD			EXCEL-LENT
0	1	2	3	4	5	6	7	8	9	10

RATING

Overall opinion of book .... _____
Plot/Story .... _____
Setting/Location .... _____
Writing Style .... _____
Character Development .... _____
Conclusion/Ending .... _____
Scene on Front Cover .... _____

3. On average about how many books do you buy for yourself each month? _____

4. How would you classify yourself as a reader of SF/Fantasy?
   I am a ( ) light ( ) medium ( ) heavy reader.

5. What is your education?
   ( ) High School (or less) ( ) 4 yrs. college
   ( ) 2 yrs. college ( ) Post Graduate

6. Age _____ 7. Sex: ( ) Male ( ) Female

8. Please Print Name:_____

Address:_____

City: _____ State: _____ Zip: _____

Phone #: ( )_____

Thank you. Please send to New American Library, Research Dept., 1633 Broadway, New York, NY 10019.

JOIN THE *GAMING MAGI* READERS' PANEL

Help us bring you more of the books you like by filling out this survey and mailing it in today.

1. Book Title: _____
   Book #: _____

2. Using the scale below, how would you rate this book on the following features?

POOR	NOT SO GOOD			O.K.			GOOD		EXCELLENT	
0	1	2	3	4	5	6	7	8	9	10

RATING

Overall opinion of book .... _____
Plot/Story .... _____
Setting/Location .... _____
Writing Style .... _____
Character Development .... _____
Conclusion/Ending .... _____
Scene on Front Cover .... _____

3. On average about how many books do you buy for yourself each month? _____

4. How would you classify yourself as a reader of SF/Fantasy? I am a ( ) light ( ) medium ( ) heavy reader.

5. What is your education?
   ( ) High School (or less) ( ) 4 yrs. college
   ( ) 2 yrs. college ( ) Post Graduate

6. Age _____ 7. Sex: ( ) Male ( ) Female

8. Please Print Name: _____

   Address: _____

   City: _____ State: _____ Zip: _____

   Phone #: ( ) _____

Thank you. Please send to New American Library, Research Dept., 1633 Broadway, New York, NY 10019.

About the Author

DAVID F. BISCHOFF was born December 15, 1951, in Washington, D.C., and grew up in the D.C. suburbs carousing with Air Force brats near Andrews AFB. He graduated from the University of Maryland in 1973 with a B.A. in TV and Film and worked for six years with NBC Washington, then became a full-time free-lance writer.

He has written a number of novels, including *Night-world*, *Star Fall*, *Mandala*, *Day of the Dragonstar* (with Thomas F. Monteleone), *The Selkie* (with Charles Sheffield; available in a Signet edition), and the upcoming *Infinite Battle* and *Cosmos Computer*. *The Destiny Dice*, Book one of two volumes of *The Gaming Magi* is also available in a Signet edition.

His short work has appeared in such magazines as *Omni*, *Analog*, *Fantasy & Science Fiction*, and *Amazing*, as well as a number of original anthologies.

He has served as both secretary and vice-president of the Science Fiction Writers of America.

Bischoff loves movies, rock and British folk, and other things too humorous to mention. He now lives in Silver Spring, Maryland.